DEVIL'S MARSH

Devil's Marsh

CAROL A CAMPBELL

To My Mom & Dad

*Here's To Chasing Dreams &
Finding My Way Back Home!*

Prologue

Have you ever had a sick feeling in the pit of your stomach? The kind that twists and turns, gnawing at you, whispering that something's wrong? I've had that feeling before, but nothing like the day I left New Orleans. It was supposed to be a fresh start—Bayou Vista, quiet and off the map, nothing like the chaos I'd grown used to. I thought it would be peaceful. Healing, even. I should have known better.

There's something about the air here. It clings to your skin, thick and damp, like it's trying to pull you into the earth. The locals don't talk about it, not directly. They just glance at you with that knowing look, like they expect you to figure it out on your own. The warnings are in their silence, in the way they avoid the marsh, in the way their voices drop when you ask about the house.

I didn't want to believe them. I didn't *need* to believe them.

But the house... that house. The moment I stepped inside, it felt like someone—something—was watching me. At first, I convinced myself it was just the isolation. The unfamiliar creaks, the way the shadows seemed to stretch and twist as the sun set. I tried to brush it off as nerves, adjusting to a new place. But deep down, I knew.

There are some things you can't explain away. Like the cold spots that appear in the middle of a warm room. The whispers that seem to echo just below the edge of hearing. Or the way your reflection in the mirror doesn't always look quite... right.

I thought I could handle it. I've always been logical, practical, the type who doesn't believe in ghost stories. But logic doesn't help when you wake up in the middle of the night and hear footsteps in the hall, only to find no one there. Or when you find things moved—subtle at first, then more obvious. Like the house is trying to tell you something, trying to see if you're paying attention.

There's one place that everyone seems to know: *Micky's Magical Things.* The shop sits quietly on the edge of town, filled with peculiar objects, the kind that make you wonder where they came from—and who might have owned them before. Micky himself, with his rich English accent and a humble way of describing himself as "nothing, a nobody, just an old gypsy boy," is an enigma. He claims to be ordinary, but I soon discovered he was much more than that. People in town say he can talk to the other side, that he has a gift, and it's hard not to believe them once you've stepped into his shop. There's an energy there, something alive beneath the surface. He sees things others can't, but there's something else about him—something he's not telling. It's like the weight of the world rests on his shoulders, and I have a feeling that whatever's waiting for me in Bayou Vista, Micky already knows how it ends.

And Billy. I don't know what to make of him. He came out of nowhere, always just showing up when I least expect it. There's something about him that pulls me in, but at the same time, makes me question everything I know. He feels *too* perfect, like a puzzle piece that fits where it shouldn't. I tell myself it's just paranoia, but that sick feeling in my gut won't go away. It's growing stronger, like a warning I can't shake.

I thought moving here would give me a chance to start over. But now... now I'm not even sure I'll make it out. Whatever's lurking in the shadows here... it's not just watching. It's waiting. And deep down, I can't shake the feeling it's been waiting for *me* all along.

My name is Isabella Crown—Izzy if you're feeling friendly, or daring—and this is how it all unraveled.

~ 1 ~

HERE TO STAY

I shouldn't have left New Orleans, at least that's what my gut told me as I merged onto the highway. But after everything I'd been through, staying felt like I was chaining myself to a life I no longer wanted.

I still remember the day everything changed. I was just ten years old when my parents died in that car accident, and it felt like my whole world shattered. After that, Uncle James took me in, raised me as best he could, but things were never the same.

All my friends, my whole life, was in that town. But then I met Trevor. At first, he seemed like my way out, but his controlling nature pushed everyone else away. People started to distance themselves, whispering behind my back, like I was the one who had changed.

Most of my free time was spent taking care of Uncle James as he slipped further into Alzheimer's. It was heartbreaking to watch the man who raised me fade away. When his care became too much, I had no choice but to put him in a nursing home and sell my dad's estate—the home where Uncle James and I had so many memories. It was the hardest thing I've ever done.

So, I ignored the feeling—just like I'd ignored the others before it, the one that gnawed away in the pit of my stomach, begging me to stay—and kept driving, my brand-new Corvette purring beneath me. The car was my ticket to freedom, a final gift from my dad's estate, just like the house in Devil's Marsh—both paid for by an inheritance that gave me this fresh start.

As I pulled into Bayou Vista, the world seemed to slow down, or at least it felt that way. Eyes followed my car like I'd rolled in with flashing lights, the bold letters **IZZY** gleaming from my personalized license plate. I didn't mind the attention. After everything, maybe a little bit of attention wasn't the worst thing in the world. My father always told me to embrace life's moments, even the uncomfortable ones. The heat of the day pressed against the windows, and I spotted a quaint coffee shop —*Bayou Bliss.*

I parked and stepped out, my heels clicking against the pavement. As soon as I pushed open the door, the cool air hit my skin, along with the scent of roasted coffee. The place had a cozy, inviting charm—the kind that made you want to lose yourself in a good book or, in my case, a fresh start. It was time to make my first impression.

Inside, a group of women sat at a round table near the window, their conversation halting the moment I walked in. I could feel their eyes appraising me, much like they had the car. I took a breath and approached the counter, but before I could order, one of them spoke.

"Nice ride," a woman with striking red nails said, her voice dripping with curiosity. She was the first to speak, and I appreciated her boldness. What stood out most was her bright smile, full of energy and warmth, set against her deep brown skin, instantly putting me at ease. "I'm Brenda, by the way. Brenda Menifee. I'm the owner of this place." she added, gesturing proudly around the cozy coffee shop. There was something magnetic about her, a confidence that made me feel like I could trust her immediately, even in this new and unfamiliar town.

"Thanks," I replied, giving her a small smile. "Just got it."

"You've got half the town talking already," another chimed in with a laugh. Her demeanor was light and approachable, with an easy charm. "I'm Gail Terry," she added, offering a warm smile.

The group laughed, but not in a mean way. More like they'd found their way into my story already, and now they were just waiting for the details. I glanced around, sensing their curiosity growing. The others followed suit, introducing themselves one by one. The one with the bubbly personality was Shannon Wright, and next to her sat Patricia Noack, who gave me a polite smile, but I could tell she was studying me closely. Melissa Staggs rounded out the group, her posture stiff, but her eyes filled with quiet observation.

"What brings you to our little town?" Shannon asked, leaning forward with a grin. "Not many people move here without a reason."

"I needed a change," I said, keeping it simple. "Figured Bayou Vista might be a good place to start fresh."

"Fresh starts are always good," Brenda said, crossing her legs with interest. "Where you staying?"

I hesitated for a moment but saw no point in hiding it. "I bought a house out in Devil's Marsh."

A silence fell over the table, and all of their smiles dimmed, just a little. They tried to cover it up, but I noticed the way their eyes flickered between each other.

"You bought *that* place?" Patricia finally spoke, her voice cautious. "I didn't even know it was up for sale again. It's been empty for a couple of years."

"I got a great deal on it," I said, leaning against the counter. "The house is massive, like a mansion almost. It's perfect."

"Perfect?" Shannon raised an eyebrow. "Not many folks would call that place perfect."

"Really," Melissa muttered under her breath, exchanging a glance with Shannon.

Gail tilted her head, curiosity flickering in her eyes. "That house has quite a history."

"What do you mean?" I asked, curious now. I could feel a shift in the air as they exchanged glances again.

"Well," Melissa leaned forward, her voice lowering just a touch. "The last owners left one day and never came back. Just vanished. No one really knows why."

"They just vanished?" I asked, trying to keep the skepticism from my voice. They all nodded, but no one seemed eager to say more.

They weren't telling me everything; I could sense it in the way their voices grew quieter, more measured. But I wasn't about to push them. I'd only been here five minutes, and Bayou Vista seemed like the kind of place where secrets floated in the air, ready to catch you if you weren't careful.

"Don't let us scare you, darling," Brenda purred, breaking the tension with a smile. "If you need anything, we're here. Small town, you know how it is."

"Thanks," I said, still feeling their eyes on me as I shifted my weight, unsure of what to make of their sudden change in tone. "You can call me Izzy, by the way."

"You can call me Shanster," Shannon chimed in with a grin, standing up and handing me a card. "If you ever plan a vacation or just want to grab a cup of coffee, or need someone to show you around, come see me. I own *Shanster Travels*." She winked, her easy charm breaking the tension in the room and making me feel a bit more comfortable.

I smiled back, grateful for the warmth, but still aware of the cautious glances exchanged between the others. "Thanks," I repeated, feeling their eyes on me as I slowly made my way toward the door. The group offered polite smiles and small waves as I stepped out.

Once outside, I immediately noticed two men standing by my car, both clearly impressed. One had a badge clipped to his belt—likely the Sheriff—and the other looked more official, maybe the Mayor.

The Sheriff nodded as I approached. "Nice car," he said, extending a hand. "Sheriff Emmett Johnson. You must be new in town."

"Yeah, just arrived," I said, shaking his hand.

"We could tell," the other man chimed in with a chuckle. "Mayor Steve Strittmatter. We don't see many folks with a ride like this around here."

"Well, get used to it," I joked, sliding into the driver's seat. "I'm here to stay."

As I pulled out of town and headed toward the outskirts, my thoughts circled back to the women at Bayou Bliss. They knew something about Devil's Marsh they weren't saying. I wasn't naive enough to think I'd gotten the full story. The way they reacted... it was more than just small-town gossip. Something about Devil's Marsh felt... right, even if the rest of the town didn't think so.

The road out to the marsh grew narrower, and the landscape around me shifted. The trees thickened, their branches arching overhead like claws. The air felt different out here—heavier, older, as though time itself moved more slowly. Finally, my destination came into view.

The house stood like a giant, looming over the marshland—dark brick, weathered but not broken. It was grand, more than grand. It was a mansion, just like I'd said.

The towering pillars at the entrance framed a massive wooden door, blackened with age and adorned with intricate carvings I couldn't quite make out from where I stood. The front steps were cracked, worn from decades of footsteps, and thick vines climbed the walls, wrapping themselves around the corners like the marsh itself was trying to pull the house back into the earth.

I took a deep breath as I stepped out of the car. Despite the eerie atmosphere, I felt... calm. Like the house was waiting for me. The large, arched windows shimmered in the midday sun, and the front door creaked as I opened it, the sound echoing in the silence around me.

Inside, the air was cool and musty, the smell of old wood and forgotten memories filling my senses. The grand staircase stretched up into the shadows, and tall ceilings gave the place a cathedral-like feel. Dust clung to every surface, but beneath it all, I could sense the beauty—the craftsmanship of another era.

And yet, despite its grandeur, there was something else. Something just out of sight, lurking behind the walls, beneath the floorboards. The kind of feeling that told me this house held stories—stories it wasn't ready to reveal just yet.

Whatever they were, I couldn't shake the sensation that I was meant to be here. The house had chosen me, just as much as I had chosen it.

~ 2 ~

NO PLACE LIKE HOME

I stood in the center of my new home, staring up at the high ceilings, letting my eyes drift over the antique paintings and the grand staircase spiraling up to the second floor. The movers had just arrived and were busy efficiently placing my belongings where I had directed, while I remained rooted in place, taking it all in.

Most of the house was already furnished, with old, stately pieces left behind by its previous owners. The furniture, worn and antique, looked as though it had been there for decades, like a permanent part of the house's history. I was oddly grateful for it—the way those aged, creaky chairs and heavy wooden tables gave the house a strange, timeless charm. It felt less like I was moving in and more like I was stepping into someone else's life, caught in the echoes of another time.

After unpacking the last box, I wandered through the mansion, feeling both awe and unease. Every creak of the floor, every whisper of wind outside seemed louder in the quietness of the marsh. My footsteps echoed through the vast, empty halls, bouncing off the dark wood floors and faded tapestries. The air inside was thick and heavy, like it hadn't been disturbed in years.

I paused in front of an old painting at the bottom of the stairs. The subject—a woman with hollow eyes and a stern expression—seemed to follow me as I moved. A shiver ran down my spine, and I quickly turned away.

"This place could definitely use a brighter touch," I muttered to myself, though part of me kind of liked the haunted aesthetic.

The movers had finished their work quickly, disappearing down the long driveway without so much as a goodbye. Alone now, the isolation settled in.

I needed a break, so I made myself a cup of coffee. The scent of it filled the kitchen, offering some comfort against the mustiness of the house. I stepped out onto the back patio, looking out over the marsh. It stretched on endlessly before me, a tangle of murky water and twisted trees that seemed to wrap around the house like some living thing.

As I sipped my coffee, I scanned the thick fog rolling in over the marsh. It crept toward the house slowly, like ghostly fingers. It was eerie, sure, but there was something strangely beautiful about it. Then that feeling hit me. The hairs on the back of my neck stood up, and a cold shiver passed through me. I felt like I was being watched.

Slowly, I turned my head to glance behind me. My heart was racing, half-expecting to see someone—or something—standing there. But there was nothing.

I tried to shake the feeling off. "It's just nerves," I whispered to myself. I was still adjusting to this new place.

I pulled out my phone, remembering I promised Donna I'd call. Dialing her number, I waited while it rang.

"Girl, you made it?" Donna's familiar voice came through the line, and instantly I felt a little calmer.

Donna had always been my best friend, ever since we met in New Orleans. She was the only one Trevor couldn't run off, no matter how hard he tried. While everyone else slowly distanced themselves because of his controlling grip, Donna stood firm. She saw through him from the start, never afraid to call him out or stand by me when things got tough. No matter how bad things got, Donna never left my side, and hearing her voice now reminded me that I wasn't completely alone.

"Yeah, I'm here. The place is... bigger than I expected. Creepy as hell, though," I said, trying to laugh it off. "It's perfect for me—no one around for miles."

"That sounds creepy as hell," Donna teased, but I could hear the concern in her voice. "You sure you're okay out there?"

"Yeah," I said, even though I didn't quite believe it myself. "It's what I needed. A fresh start."

We talked for a while longer, but the feeling of being watched didn't leave me. Every now and then, I glanced around, expecting to catch a glimpse of something—or someone—lurking just out of sight.

That night, after the sun set, the house felt different. The wind howled against the old windows, and every creak and groan seemed louder, more ominous. The faint smell of mildew clung to the air, and the shadows seemed to stretch across the walls, twisting into strange shapes.

I tried to relax. I poured myself a glass of wine and curled up on the old leather couch with a book I'd found on one of the dusty shelves. As I brushed off the cover, my heart skipped a beat—*Devil Worship: Ancient Rituals and Dark Secrets*. The title sent a chill down my spine, but I opened it anyway, curiosity getting the better of me. Still, every gust of wind rattling the windows made my heart jump, and I found myself reading the same sentence over and over again without taking it in.

I couldn't shake the unease the book on devil worshipping stirred in me, so I quickly closed it and shoved it back onto the shelf, the dust swirling in the dim light. My fingers brushed against another book, this one smaller, leather-bound, and worn from time. I pulled it out carefully—*Journal of Mary LaBlanc* was etched faintly on the cover. As I opened it, delicate, faded handwriting filled the pages. Mary spoke of her deep love for the house, how it had been passed down through generations of her family since the 1800s. She called herself 'the queen' of the estate, vowing she would never leave. Each word carried a strange sense of possession, as if she still lingered here, watching over her kingdom.

I couldn't stop reading, even as the house creaked around me, the old wooden beams groaning in the quiet. Then, the doorbell rang. Startled, I looked at the clock—it was **3:33**.

I froze, my book slipping from my hands. Who could be out here at this hour? My first thought was Donna, but she lived too far away. No one else knew I was here.

My heart pounded as I stood up. The hallway to the front door seemed to stretch endlessly before me, each step growing heavier with dread. When I reached the door, I hesitated, straining to hear any sound.

Nothing.

I peeked through the peephole—no one was there. The porch light flickered weakly, barely penetrating the dense mist that seemed to swallow the front steps. There was no sign of anyone.

"Hello?" I called out, my voice trembling.
Silence.

I took a deep breath and unlocked the door, opening it just a crack. Cool, damp air drifted in, swirling around my feet. I hesitated, then swung the door wider and stepped forward, scanning the yard.

"Hello? Is anyone there?" I called again.
Still nothing. The yard and driveway were completely hidden, the white haze stretching endlessly into the night.

I quickly shut the door and locked it, leaning against it as my pulse raced. I reached for my phone, thinking about calling Donna again, but before I could, I heard something—glass clinking, like something had fallen over.

The noise came from the kitchen.

I wasn't alone.

I set the phone down and moved slowly, my breath quickening. The house felt colder now, darker. The creaking floorboards seemed louder under my feet. I reached the kitchen door, heart hammering in my chest.

"Hello?" I whispered, but there was no answer.

I flipped on the light. The kitchen was empty. The only thing out of place was shattered glass scattered across the floor, as if it had been knocked off the counter.

I knelt down to pick up the pieces, holding them in my hands as I stared at the empty room. Had it fallen on its own? Or had someone knocked it over?

The lights flickered suddenly, plunging me into darkness. I froze, my breath catching in my throat.

Tap. Tap. Tap.

The sound came from the back door. A slow, deliberate tapping, like someone gently knocking on the glass.

I felt my stomach drop. Slowly, I turned to look at the sliding glass door that led out to the backyard. The fog pressed against the glass, but just beyond it, I could see a faint outline - a figure, standing there, watching.

My breath quickened. I backed away from the door, my heart pounding. The tapping continued, harder now, more urgent.

I grabbed my phone, but before I could dial, the tapping stopped.

Silence.

I didn't move. I couldn't. My eyes stayed locked on the door, waiting for something, anything, to happen.

Then the doorbell rang again. This time, it was louder, more insistent.

I rushed to the front door, yanked it open—again, nothing. No one was there. The fog wrapped around the porch like a thick blanket, making it impossible to see beyond the yard.

But then, just at the edge of the marsh, I saw it again—a figure, standing perfectly still, watching me.

I blinked, and it was gone.

Heart pounding, I slammed the door shut and locked it tight. My hands were shaking, my body trembling. Something was wrong with this place. Someone—or something—was out there.

A cold certainty washed over me—I wasn't alone.

~ 3 ~

WHISPERS OF THE PAST

I felt like I hadn't slept at all. My eyes were heavy, and my mind swirled with thoughts of what had happened just hours before—the figure, the cold spots, the creaking noises. I kept telling myself it couldn't have been real, but the fear still clung to me like a second skin.

Dragging myself out of bed, I made a cup of coffee, hoping it would jolt me back to reality. As I sipped, I stared out the kitchen window, but my thoughts were elsewhere. The house was eerie in the daylight too, but at least the sun gave me some comfort. Today, I decided to take a closer look upstairs. Maybe it would help me make sense of the strange feelings this place gave me.

I climbed the stairs, passing that damn portrait of the woman with the cold eyes. It had been hanging downstairs before the staircase, and I couldn't stand looking at her anymore.

"I'm definitely replacing you today," I muttered, stepping back down and ripping the frame from the wall. The back was scratched with the initials *M.L.* I paused, staring at the letters. What the hell could that stand for? Then it hit me—*Mary LaBlanc*, the name from the journal. A chill ran down my spine as I propped the portrait against the wall, her stern eyes seeming to follow my every move. Trying to shake the unsettling feeling, I quickly turned away and kept moving.

The hallway felt longer than before, the carpet worn under my feet. When I reached the last room, I stopped. The door was slightly ajar, and something about it felt untouched. I pushed it open and stepped inside. The air was stale, thick with dust and time.

The bedroom looked like it hadn't been disturbed in decades. Everything was perfectly in place but old—frozen in time. There, on the nightstand, was a tarnished silver picture frame. I picked it up, my stomach dropping when I saw her face again. The same woman from the portrait downstairs, her gaze even colder in this photograph.

A shiver crawled up my spine. This whole house seemed haunted by her.

As I put the frame back, something caught my eye. Movement. I turned sharply toward the mirror—and for a brief second, I swore I saw her standing there, staring at me.

I gasped, stepping back, my heart racing. "No, no, no."

When I blinked, she was gone. It was just my wide-eyed reflection staring back at me. My pulse pounded in my ears, and sweat gathered on the back of my neck.

Get a grip, Izzy. It's just your imagination.

But even as I tried to convince myself, I couldn't shake the feeling that something was deeply wrong with this house. I needed answers—answers that clearly weren't going to come from poking around here.

By the time I made it to town, I was desperate for a normal conversation—anything to take my mind off the strange things I'd seen—but I knew I needed more answers. The unease clung to me like a shadow, growing heavier with every step. Whatever was happening in that house wasn't just in my head, and pretending everything was fine wasn't going to help.

I parked near *Burning Love*, the lingerie shop I'd passed the day before. Maybe someone here would know something. Inside, the shop was warm and inviting, with soft lighting and vibrant displays. A woman behind the counter greeted me with a friendly smile, her blonde hair pulled back into a messy bun.

"Hey there! I'm Cindy Blevins," she said, her voice bright and welcoming, with a slight northern accent. "What can I help you with today?"

"Just browsing," I said, trying to sound casual, but my voice trembled enough that Cindy noticed.

"You alright, hon?" she asked, her smile softening into something more genuine.

I hesitated for a second, then let out a long breath. "I just moved into the old house in Devil's Marsh."

Her expression shifted, the brightness in her eyes dimming slightly. "Oh, I see." She paused, as if choosing her words carefully. "That's... quite the place."

I forced a laugh. "You're not the first person to say that."

"Yeah, I'm new in town too, so I don't know much," Cindy said with a shrug. "But I've heard some rumors about that place."

"What kind of rumors?" I asked, leaning in.

"I don't want to spread lies. You should stop by *Pearl & Crystal Cove*. Gail, Patricia, and Margie run it—they've been here forever. If anyone knows the truth, it's them."

"I actually met them yesterday, but they didn't say much about the house," I admitted.

"Small towns are weird like that," Cindy said with a knowing nod. "I wish I could help more. But hey, if you ever want to grab lunch, coffee, or catch a movie, just let me know. I'm always around."

I thanked her and left, the door's bell jingling behind me as I stepped back onto the street. The pleasant warmth of the shop quickly faded as I walked toward the *Sheriff's office*. If I couldn't get information from the locals, maybe the Sheriff could help me.

But when I arrived, the Sheriff wasn't there. One of the deputies, a young guy with an overly polite smile, said he could take a message.

"It's not a big deal," I told him. "I just have a few questions. I'll catch him when I see him."

As I stepped back outside, I spotted a man across the street. He stood in front of *Micky's Magical Things*, casually drinking coffee, but his eyes were locked on me. A jolt of unease shot through me as I tightened my grip on my bag. His gaze didn't waver—it was as if he knew something I didn't.

My heart raced. Who the hell is that?

Trying to keep my panic at bay, I hurried to my car, avoiding eye contact. My heart pounded as I slipped into the driver's seat, shutting the door behind me with a shaky breath. Without a second glance, I started the engine and drove off.

Next, I found myself at the *library*. Maybe they had some records, something that could explain the unsettling history of the house. As I approached the counter, a woman greeted me with a polite smile.

"Hi, I'm Terrie Lawson. Can I help you?"

"I hope so," I said, forcing a smile. "I'm Izzy. I just moved here. I bought the house out in Devil's Marsh."

The librarian's face paled a bit. "Oh," she muttered, clearly uncomfortable. "Lena? Can you come here?"

Another woman approached, her eyes narrowing slightly as she took me in.

"What's the issue?"

"She bought the house in Devil's Marsh," the librarian said in a hushed voice, as if I couldn't hear.

I sighed. "Why does everyone get weird when I mention that house?"

Lena gave me a sad smile. "It's got a... history."

I folded my arms, feeling my patience wear thin. "What kind of history?"

Lena leaned closer, her voice lowering. "Fifty years ago, a man with his face painted like a clown murdered his family in that house—his sister, his brothers, and his mother. People who've bought the place since then... they disappear."

My stomach twisted. The realtor had told me about the murders, but she said it happened outside the house, in the marsh. *So, did she lie?* "Disappear? Like, they just left?"

"No. No one knows what happened to them. No bodies. No signs of life. Just... gone."

My mind raced. I'd heard urban legends before, but this felt different—like there was something dark hiding beneath the surface.

Trying to shake off the growing unease, I grabbed some food to-go from *Tanya's Crawfish Shack*. As I waited for my order, I struck up a conversation with Tanya. She seemed friendly enough, and I hoped she wouldn't shut me out like the others had when I mentioned I owned the house in the marsh.

"Looks like business is good here," I said, trying to ease into the small-town friendliness I was craving.

Tanya smiled as she wiped her hands on a towel. "We do alright. Bayou Vista's got its regulars. You're new around here, right?"

"Yeah," I replied, forcing a smile. "Moved into the house in Devil's Marsh."

Tanya raised an eyebrow, her smile widening. "Ah, that explains the whispers. Bayou Vista's rumor mill is always turning," she said with a grin. "People talk, especially about that house you bought."

I forced a laugh. "Yeah, I've noticed."

"They've got some wild theories," she said, leaning on the counter. "Especially with all the women who've gone missing."

"Missing women?"

"Four or five a year," Tanya explained. "No one knows who's behind it. People used to think it was Roy, Loretta Cobb's stepdad, but he's dead, and the disappearances haven't stopped. There've been so many different rumors over the years... some folks even say it's tied to that clown who murdered his family—the one who lived in your house."

I felt a chill creep down my spine. "And people still believe that?"

Tanya shrugged. "Some do. They say he's still out there, but I don't know. He'd have to be what? Ninety by now?"

I let out a laugh, but it felt empty, lacking any real humor.

"If you want more details, you could talk to Loretta. She owns *Heavenly Wishes*—just opened it recently. She's lived here her whole life, so she might know more about your house's history," Tanya suggested.

"Thank you," I smiled politely, taking the food from Tanya's hands. "I might do that."

There were still too many questions swirling in my head—and not nearly enough answers.

The drive home passed in a blur, my mind spinning with everything I'd learned. As I pulled up to the end of the long driveway, I stayed in the car for a moment, staring at the house. Its dark silhouette loomed against the fading light of the setting sun, an unsettling presence that seemed to watch me back.

My thoughts raced—stories of murders, disappearances, and the strange things I'd already seen.

I gripped the steering wheel tighter, my knuckles turning white, as the wind howled through the trees, carrying faint whispers I couldn't quite make out.

I knew I wasn't alone. And whatever was watching me—it was only just beginning.

~ 4 ~

THE UNRAVELING

I woke up gasping for breath, my skin damp with sweat, and my heart pounding in my chest. The images from the nightmare clung to me—endless hallways, walls closing in, and those whispers. Always the whispers. They followed me wherever I turned, growing louder with every step, the walls pressing closer as I ran.

But as I sat up, a chill crept over me. Something was wrong. The bed felt different—the room, different. My eyes darted around, and it hit me: I wasn't in my bedroom.

Panic surged through me as I realized I had no memory of leaving my room. I was in one of the other bedrooms upstairs, one I hadn't explored yet. *Was I sleepwalking?* I thought, my pulse racing. It wasn't out of the norm for me—I'd had episodes of sleepwalking before—but never anything like this. I couldn't breathe for a moment, staring at the unfamiliar furniture, trying to make sense of it. How had I gotten here?

I stood, my legs shaky as I pulled myself together. *It's stress,* I told myself, rubbing my face. *New house, new town, all this talk about the house's past...* But that didn't stop the tightness in my chest or the cold prickle running down my spine. I hurried back down to my room, half-expecting to hear footsteps following me.

I decided to keep busy, hoping that cleaning the rooms might distract me from the unsettling feeling that seemed to linger in every corner of the house. I grabbed a dust rag and some cleaner, starting with the bedroom and working my way down the hall. But as the day wore on, the strange occurrences only grew more intense.

At first, it was just faint tapping at the windows, like something brushing against the glass. But each time I checked, there was nothing there—no wind, no movement, just an eerie stillness outside. Then came the footsteps. They were light at first, almost faint, like someone pacing above me in the attic. I tried to brush it off—*old houses creak,* I reasoned. *This is just the house settling.*

But the footsteps grew louder, more deliberate, as if something was making its way through the halls. My breath hitched, and I stood frozen, my phone in hand, ready to call someone—anyone. The sound stopped. Silence. I let out a shaky breath, trying to convince myself I was overreacting. *It's just the house,* I thought again, more forcefully this time.

But doubt crept in. *Or is it?* my mind whispered. *What if it's not?*

I decided to stop cleaning and search the house. If I was going to live here, I needed to know every corner of this place. Maybe if I explored, I'd stop imagining things.

In the living room, I rummaged through old drawers and cabinets. Most were filled with the kind of junk you'd expect—old letters, dusty knickknacks—but then I found it: a small, leather-bound journal hidden at the back of a side table.

The journal looked worn, its edges frayed, but it didn't feel old. As I opened it, a faint scent of roses drifted up, unexpected and out of place, confirming that this journal wasn't as old as it first seemed. The fragrance felt too fresh, too recent, as though it had been handled not long ago. The early entries were nothing remarkable, simple reflections of daily life from someone named Anna. But the further I read, the more the tone shifted. The writing became erratic, the letters slanting wildly, as though written in a frenzy. Each line seemed more unhinged than the last, almost desperate, and fear that clung to the pages like a hidden warning.

"The house is different at night. I hear them—footsteps, whispers. They're watching me. I can feel it."

My fingers tightened on the page, my heart pounding in my ears as I turned to the next entry.

"There are figures in the marsh at night. Their faces... their faces are painted like clowns. If I blink, they're gone, but I know they're real. I know what I saw."

A shiver ran through me, and I almost closed the journal. But something compelled me to keep reading.

"The mirror... it shows things. Not reflections. Something else. I'm afraid to look."

The final entry sent an icy chill down my spine.

"It's watching me... I can feel it... but the marsh, that's the key. If only—"

The rest of the page had been torn out.

I stared at the jagged edges, my breath catching in my throat. The mirror. I knew exactly which mirror she was talking about. The one upstairs—the one I couldn't bring myself to look at directly. My skin prickled with unease, and I stood there for a moment, clutching the journal to my chest as the house seemed to close in around me.

I made my way upstairs, my legs heavy with dread. The mirror loomed in the bedroom at the end of the hall-way, its old frame tarnished with age. I could feel the air shift as I approached, a chill settling over me.

It's just a mirror, I told myself. *Stop being ridiculous.*

I reached out, my hand trembling as my fingers grazed the surface. A cold, electric sensation shot through me, and I jerked my hand back, heart pounding. It was like something beneath the glass had reached out and touched me, something cold and alive. I stepped back, my chest heaving as my mind reeled. *This isn't real. It's just the house messing with me,* I thought, but I couldn't shake the feeling that the mirror was watching me, wait-ing for me to make a mistake.

I tried to laugh it off, but the sound came out hollow, and I turned away quickly, not daring to look at my re-flection. Out of the corner of my eye, I thought I saw movement in the glass—something shifting just beyond my line of sight—but I refused to turn back. *Don't look,* I thought. *Just don't look.*

By evening, I needed to escape the suffocating walls of the house. I drove into town, my mind still racing from the journal, the footsteps, and the mirror. I parked outside *Heavenly Wishes*, hoping for a conversation that might ease my mind. Inside, the smell of lavender and old wood filled the air, and Loretta greeted me with a polite smile.

"Hi," I said, forcing a smile of my own as I approached her. "I'm Izzy. I just moved into the house out in Devil's Marsh."

Loretta's smile faltered slightly, her eyes flicking toward the door as if checking for someone. "Oh... that house." Her voice dropped, and I felt a flicker of dread settle in my chest.

I nodded, sensing her discomfort. "Yeah. I've already heard about the disappearances—the rumors are hard to miss. I just don't know what to do."

"Well," Loretta began, "for starters, I'd have Preacher John come out and bless your house. He's usually over at St. Theresa's Church. That place, though... it has a way of stirring up all kinds of dark stories. And let me tell you, those stories? They're more than just rumors."

I leaned in slightly, my curiosity piqued. "More to them?"

Loretta hesitated, glancing around the shop as if she didn't want to be overheard. "Yes, but if anyone can help you, it's Micky."

"Micky?" I asked, surprised. "From *Micky's Magical Things?*"

She nodded. "That's right. He's a great man. Every morning, he volunteers to take food and medicine out to the elderly. He's always helping those in need. And when I was dealing with my stepdad, Roy, Micky was there for me. I don't know what I would've done without him." Her eyes softened as she glanced around. "This is what *Heavenly Wishes* is all about—giving back, lifting up those who need it most. Whether it's helping families through hard times or just offering a bit of hope, this center has become a lifeline for so many. It's more than just a place; it's a reminder that no one has to face their struggles alone."

I raised an eyebrow. "What happened with Roy?"

Her eyes darkened slightly as she spoke. "Roy wasn't the man everyone thought he was. He was abusive, controlling. For years, I lived in fear of him, and no one knew what was really happening. But Micky noticed something was wrong. He never stopped helping me, and if it wasn't for him, I don't know how I would've gotten through it."

"I'll keep him in mind, but first, I'll contact the preacher." Izzy smiled.

Loretta gave a knowing nod. "He's not just a shopkeeper. If anyone can help you figure out what's going on with that house, it's Micky."

I nodded, appreciating her advice. "Thank you, Loretta. I'll reach out to him soon."

As I left *Heavenly Wishes* and headed back toward Devil's Marsh, Loretta's words echoed in my mind. *Micky wasn't just a shopkeeper—he was the one who could help me uncover the truth behind everything that had been haunting me since I moved in.*

The drive back from town felt different. Night had fully settled in, and the road seemed darker, narrower than before. I tried to focus on the stretch of pavement ahead, but the uneasy feeling gnawed at me, stronger now after what Loretta had said.

I parked at the edge of my long driveway, the headlights illuminating the front of the house. My breath caught in my throat. There, standing by the window—just for a split second—I saw a figure, unmoving, watching.

It can't be real. I blinked. Gone.

I sat frozen, gripping the steering wheel, my eyes glued to the window. *Did I really see that?* I asked myself, my heart pounding so hard it echoed in my ears. I shook my head, trying to clear it, but the doubt lingered.

I stepped out of the car slowly, forcing myself to breathe. As I walked toward the house, every instinct screamed at me to turn around, get back in the car, and drive away. But I couldn't—I had to know. My hands trembled as I reached for the front door. The air felt colder, heavier as I stepped inside.

The house was still, too still. The kind of silence that made every creak, every subtle noise feel amplified. As I moved toward the stairs, the sound of my footsteps echoed softly, and I realized the front door had quietly closed behind me—on its own.

No. I spun around, my pulse racing. There was no breeze, no reason for the door to move. My fingers twitched toward the handle, but then I heard it.

A faint, low whisper.

It came from upstairs, followed by the unmistakable sound of a door creaking open.

I stood paralyzed for a moment, heart racing, unsure of whether I should move forward or run. I swallowed hard, forcing myself to listen. The whispering grew louder, unintelligible but unmistakable.

You're overreacting, I tried to convince myself, taking one shaky step toward the stairs. *You're hearing things. There's no such thing as ghosts.*

But then, out of the corner of my eye, I saw it—the same figure, standing at the top of the staircase. A shadowy silhouette, tall and still.

I froze, my breath catching in my throat as I tried to make sense of what I was seeing. The figure didn't move. My fingers tightened around the banister as I slowly took a step back. But before I could turn, the figure began to descend the stairs, one slow, deliberate step at a time.

My legs refused to move. I wanted to run, scream, do anything, but I was rooted to the spot. My chest heaved, panic coursing through me as the figure came closer and closer, its shape more defined with every step.

The last thing I saw before everything went black was a pale, painted face—like a clown, grinning at me from the shadows.

~ 5 ~

SHADOWS IN THE LIGHT

I woke up gasping, heart pounding, the sheets twisted so tightly around my legs it felt like they were trying to pin me down. My body trembled, the cold from last night clinging to my skin, despite the sunlight that spilled through the curtains. I was naked. Completely exposed. My breath hitched as I lay there, struggling to make sense of it—of *him*.

That grotesque grin, the sickening white face smeared with red, the clown... His eyes, hollow and empty, yet full of something sinister. I had seen him. And then—nothing. A void, swallowing me whole.

I rubbed my arms, desperate to feel grounded, but they weren't mine anymore. They felt like a stranger's, touched by someone else while I slept. The sensation lingered, like ghostly fingers still trailing over my skin, as if *he* had been there too—close enough to touch.

I shivered, grabbing the sheet and wrapping it around me, as if that flimsy piece of fabric could protect me from whatever had been lurking in the house. But I could feel it. Something was wrong. Something had happened, and whatever it was, it had left its mark.

I stumbled out of bed, my legs shaky, my breath ragged as I caught sight of my reflection in the mirror on the far wall. There were smudges on my skin, like dark, oily handprints, faint but unmistakable, trailing from my shoulders down to my waist. My stomach turned. What had happened to me?

I couldn't stay here, not like this. Not with the memory of those empty eyes painted like a mask staring into my soul. I threw on the first clothes I could find—a pair of jeans and a loose sweater—and hurried downstairs, my heart beating faster with every step. The house was too quiet, the air thick with the kind of stillness that felt alive. I swore I heard a whisper, faint, like the breath of someone standing just behind me. But when I turned around—nothing.

The drive into town was a blur. I couldn't get that image out of my head—the way the clown had stood there, staring at me, as if I was prey. I didn't know where else to turn, but I needed real help. Aside from Micky, the only person who came to mind was Preacher John. Growing up Catholic, I was sure he could help.

I didn't know much about him, only that Loretta had suggested getting him to bless the house. I wasn't sure what good it would do, but I had to try something. I could only hope he'd agree, despite the stories about the place.

I kept replaying the scene in my mind, over and over, trying to make sense of it. But nothing made sense anymore.

St. Theresa's Church came into view, its whitewashed walls standing out against the trees that crowded the edge of town. I parked and sat for a moment, gripping the steering wheel, trying to steady my breath. I wasn't sure what I'd tell him, or how much he'd believe. But I had to try.

Inside, the church was quiet, almost too quiet. The air smelled of old wood and incense. Preacher John was at the altar, arranging candles. He looked up when I entered, his expression calm, but I could see the curiosity in his eyes. He hadn't expected a visitor this early.

"Morning," he said, his voice deep, carrying the weight of years of sermons. "Can I help you?"

I swallowed, my throat dry. "I... I'm Izzy. Isabella Crown. I just moved into the house in Devil's Marsh."

His eyebrows lifted slightly. "That house?" His voice tightened just a bit, the words heavy with something unspoken.

I nodded. "Something happened last night. I don't know how to explain it. I saw... someone. A clown. He was in the house, and then... everything went black. When I woke up this morning, I..." I hesitated, not wanting to sound insane. "I woke up, and I was... naked. I don't remember anything after seeing him."

Preacher John stood still for a moment, then sighed, rubbing his chin. "You're not the first to say strange things happen in that house. It's been empty a long time, but the stories about it... they go way back."

"I don't know what else to do," I admitted, my voice shaking. "I thought maybe you could come... bless the house or something. Please. I can't stay there alone with whatever's inside."

He didn't speak right away. His eyes searched mine, and I could see the hesitation, the wariness. "That's a place not many folks want to go," he said quietly. "Some say there's something there, something that ain't meant for the living."

"But you're a man of faith," I pressed. "Can't you help me?"

Preacher John sighed deeply, then nodded. "Alright. I'll come with you. But I warn you, Miss Crown, I don't think a simple blessing is going to solve whatever's been stirred up in that house."

Relief washed over me, though it was tinged with fear. If even he had doubts, what was I really dealing with?

We drove in silence. The gravel road leading up to the house seemed longer this time, the trees pressing in from both sides like they were trying to block our path. When the house came into view, Preacher John's grip on the steering wheel tightened, his knuckles white.

"That's the place," he muttered, more to himself than to me.

He parked, and we stepped out. The air felt colder here, even though the sun was bright overhead. Preacher

John eyed the house, his hand resting on the Bible he had tucked under his arm.

As we approached the front door, it creaked open—on its own.

Preacher John stopped short, a low curse slipping from his lips. "Did you touch it?" he asked.

I shook my head, my heart racing. "No."

He hesitated, then took a deep breath, stepping inside. I followed, my skin prickling with unease. Inside, the house felt even more oppressive than before. The air was thick, almost choking, and the shadows seemed to dance at the edges of my vision.

Preacher John began muttering a prayer, his voice steady but low. "In the name of the Father, the Son, and the Holy Spirit, I cast out any unclean spirits that may dwell within these walls."

The room felt colder, and I shivered. I could see my breath now, hanging in the air like smoke, and the faintest sound of whispers echoed from the corners of the room. Preacher John stood in the center of the living room, holding his cross out in front of him. He continued his prayer, his voice steady but low, barely audible over the growing hum in the air. He glanced up the staircase, his eyes narrowing.

Then I saw it—something at the top of the stairs. A shadow. No, not a shadow. It was more than that. It shifted, moved, like it was watching us.

"Do you see that?" I whispered, my voice trembling.

Preacher John's jaw tightened. "I see it."

He held up his Bible, stepping forward, his voice growing louder. "In the name of Jesus Christ, I command you to leave this place!"

The shadow moved, slowly at first, then faster. It was coming down the stairs, but there was no sound. Just the growing darkness.

I stumbled back, panic rising in my chest. "John…"

But before I could say more, something reached out from the shadows—an arm, long and thin, its fingers impossibly long. It grabbed Preacher John by the arm, pulling him toward the staircase.

He cried out, struggling to free himself, his Bible falling to the floor with a dull thud. I watched, frozen in horror, as he was dragged up the stairs, his body slamming against the steps as he tried to fight back.

"Help me!" he screamed, his voice filled with terror. His cross fell from his hand, clattering to the ground.

I ran forward, but it was too late. He disappeared into the darkness at the top of the stairs, his screams echoing through the house before they were abruptly cut off.

I stood there, trembling, my breath coming in short, ragged gasps. The house had fallen into an eerie silence, but I could feel it—whatever had taken him was still here. Watching. Waiting.

I needed to leave. I needed to run. But just as I turned, the door slammed shut with a deafening bang.

Something was in this house. And it wasn't going to let us go.

~ 6 ~

THE CALM

"If I ever get out of here, I'm never coming back!" I shouted, my voice echoing through the house. My hands trembled as I fought with the front door, the cold brass knob refusing to turn no matter how hard I twisted. The air in the house had grown thick, oppressive, as if something unseen was pressing against me, urging me to stay.

Then, without warning, the atmosphere shifted.

The air became lighter, almost serene, like a breeze had swept through, carrying away the heaviness that had been weighing me down. The tension that had gripped me by the throat loosened, and suddenly, the door handle turned easily in my hand. The door creaked open, its hinges groaning softly in the quiet. I blinked in disbelief. It was as if the house had released me.

A low sound from upstairs broke the stillness, a groan that sent a shiver down my spine.

"Isabella..." The voice, weak and ragged, called my name.

I spun around, heart pounding in my chest. Preacher John. I could hear him at the top of the stairs, his voice barely more than a whisper. Panic surged through me as I rushed to the staircase, taking the steps two at a time.

When I reached him, he was lying on the floor, slowly sitting up, his face pale and drawn. Sweat slicked his brow, and he looked exhausted, like he'd just survived a battle I hadn't been there to witness.

"Preacher John, what happened?" I asked, kneeling beside him. My hands hovered near his shoulders, unsure if I should help or keep my distance.

He rubbed a hand across his face, his eyes half-lidded, as if trying to shake off whatever had just happened. "That evil... it had me. Dragged me up the stairs. I could feel it pulling me..." His voice was hoarse, raw from the screams I had heard moments before. "But now... it's gone. It just... left."

I helped him to his feet, my own legs feeling weak as I stood. The house was eerily still now, the oppressive weight from before completely gone. I looked around, expecting something—anything—to move, but everything was unnervingly calm.

I walked to the bedroom at the end of the hall, where the mirror stood—the same mirror that had once reflected the distorted, grotesque figures of the house's malevolent presence. Now, it showed only my reflection—normal, unthreatening. I reached out, pressing my fingertips to the glass, half expecting something to lunge at me from the other side.

"How can that be?" I whispered. "How can everything just... change like that?"

Preacher John limped over, wiping sweat from his brow, his breaths coming in shallow gasps. "The blessing was stronger than the evil that was here. It wasn't easy, but something... something weakened it enough for me to drive it out."

I turned to him, watching his face, trying to see if he truly believed it was over. His eyes darted around the room, never resting on any one thing for too long, as if he didn't trust the peace.

"Do you think it's really gone?" I asked, the doubt creeping into my voice.

"For now," he said quietly. "But if it comes back, you need to be ready."

He placed a hand on my shoulder as we headed toward the door. Outside, the sun bathed the front yard in a warm, golden glow, softening the edges of the landscape. The calm felt almost unnatural after the chaos inside, as if the house itself had drawn a line between the darkness within and the serene evening outside. I walked him to his truck, the tension still gnawing at me despite his re-assurances.

On the way back to St. Theresa's Church to get my car, Preacher John spoke again, his voice low and steady. "You need to understand something, Isabella. If that evil re-turns, I might not be able to help you again."

I felt a chill creep up my spine. "What do you mean?"

He tightened his grip on the steering wheel. "There's someone you should know about. Micky. He runs a shop in town, 'Micky's Magical Things.' People don't talk about it much, but he's... different. He can talk to the dead, has experience with exorcisms, and understands things most of us can't. If it ever gets bad again... you'll need him."

The rest of the ride passed in tense silence. I couldn't shake the feeling that something had shifted, that maybe the calm in the house was just a temporary reprieve. Preacher John pulled up at St. Theresa's Church, and I thanked him before getting out of the truck and walking over to my car. As I watched him drive off, his truck disappearing down the road, I took a deep breath, trying to steady my nerves.

The drive home was quiet, but the unease gnawed at me the entire way. As I neared my house, something made me stop in the middle of the street. My foot hovered over the brake as my eyes caught movement.

A man was walking down the road, tall, broad-shouldered, with the kind of presence that made the world around him seem to stop. He was the most handsome man I had ever seen, his hair dark and tousled like he'd just rolled out of bed, his eyes catching the last bit of sunlight in a way that made them gleam.

Without thinking, I approached him, my curiosity overpowering the lingering unease in my chest. "Hey," I called out, my voice more casual than I felt. "I haven't seen you around here before."

He stopped, turning toward me with a smile that was just the right amount of charming. "I'm Billy," he said smoothly. "I live up the road," he added, though he didn't offer any more details.

I tilted my head, intrigued. "I just moved here. My name is Isabella, but you can call me Izzy. I didn't think there were any houses up that way."

He chuckled, the sound deep and warm. "Not too many. It's quiet out here. I like that."

Something about his easy confidence drew me in. I knew better than to trust a stranger, especially in a place like Devil's Marsh, but there was something about him that made me feel safe. Or maybe it was just the need for something... someone... normal in the midst of all the chaos.

"You live alone?" he asked, a hint of something playful in his tone.

"For now," I said, matching his smile. "What about you?"

He shrugged, his eyes lingering on me for just a moment too long. "Yeah, I'm on my own."

My heart raced, but I managed to keep a playful smile on my face as I spoke. "So, Billy... what's your favorite meal?"

His grin widened as he met my gaze. "Why? You planning to cook for me already?"

I shrugged, trying to play it cool. "Maybe I am. But it depends—are you picky, or can you handle a little mystery?"

He chuckled, stepping closer, his eyes locked on mine. "I think I can handle a little mystery. Especially if it means spending more time with you, Izzy."

I raised an eyebrow, feeling a little thrill at the way he said my name, like it was something special. "Smooth talker. You always charm your way into dinner invitations?"

"Only when the invitation's worth it," he shot back, his voice low and teasing. He took another step toward me, and I could feel the distance between us shrinking.

I felt a flutter of excitement but tried to keep it together, tilting my head at him. "So, I'm worth it?"

Billy's eyes gleamed in the twilight. "Oh, you're more than worth it. In fact, I'd say I'm the lucky one here." His voice dipped, full of that confident flirtation that made my pulse quicken.

I couldn't help but smile. "Flattery will only get you so far, Billy."

"Well, how far are we talking?" he teased, his tone playful but with just enough edge to make my stomach flip.

I bit my lip, holding his gaze. "Far enough to see if you can handle my cooking tonight."

Billy's smile widened, and he leaned a little closer, his voice dropping to a near-whisper. "Now that sounds like a challenge. Think I'll need dessert too?"

I laughed, feeling the tension between us shift into something electric. "We'll see how dinner goes first."

His eyes flicked down to my lips for just a second before returning to meet mine. "Deal. But I've got a feeling it's going to be the best meal I've had in a long time."

I crossed my arms, feeling the warmth from our little back-and-forth. "Confident, aren't you?"

He leaned in slightly, his voice smooth. "You're the one inviting me to dinner, Izzy. Confidence must be contagious."

I gave him a playful look, stepping a little closer myself. "Fine. You bring the charm, and I'll bring the food."

Billy grinned, his eyes sparkling in the fading light. "It's a date then."

As he turned to walk away, I couldn't help but call after him, my tone flirty. "Just don't be late."

He glanced over his shoulder, giving me a wink. "Wouldn't dream of it."

I watched him disappear down the road, my heart still racing from the exchange. Inviting him over for dinner had been impulsive, reckless even. But something about the way he looked at me—the way his presence filled the space—made it feel like the right kind of risk. I couldn't shake the thought that having someone else in the house—someone real—might keep the darkness that lingered in Devil's Marsh at bay.

Later that evening, as promised, he showed up at my door, all charm and smooth politeness. We ate together in the dim glow of the kitchen, our conversation flowing easily at first. But then, as the night wore on, I started noticing little things that didn't sit right. The way his eyes never seemed to blink. The strange pauses in his speech, like he was carefully choosing each word—or worse, like he was forgetting what he was supposed to say and searching for the right thing.

But I ignored it. His looks, his charm—they were a convenient distraction from the nagging doubts at the edges of my mind. I convinced myself it was nothing. After all, I'd invited him in, hadn't I? Maybe I was just being paranoid.

When he finally left, I stood by the door, watching him walk down the driveway. That's when it struck me—he didn't have a car. I hadn't noticed that earlier, too caught up in the moment, but now it felt... odd. Who walks everywhere these days, especially out here in the middle of nowhere?

I kept watching as he turned onto the street, his tall figure illuminated by the faint glow of the moonlight. Just as he reached the corner, something strange happened—he vanished. One moment he was there, and in the blink of an eye, he was gone—the street eerily empty, as if he had never been there at all.

I slammed the door shut, my heart pounding against my chest, the unease from earlier rushing back in full force. What had I just witnessed? Had my mind played tricks on me, or was there something far more unsettling about Billy than I was willing to admit?

I stood there, frozen for a long moment, wondering if I'd made a terrible mistake by letting him in.

THE LAKE

I woke up feeling... peaceful. It was strange, after everything. For the first time since I arrived in Devil's Marsh, I didn't wake up with that heavy feeling pressing down on my chest, like I was suffocating under the weight of the town's history. The sunlight filtered gently through the curtains, casting a soft glow across the room. For a brief moment, everything seemed normal—almost serene, like the quiet before a storm.

I'd only been here less than a week, and so much had already happened. From the moment I set foot in this place, an oppressive energy clung to me, filling the house with dread. I wasn't imagining it—the evil had been cast out just yesterday. Whatever dark presence had haunted the house was gone, leaving me with this lightness, this calm.

Stretching under the covers, I allowed myself a rare smile. Maybe I hadn't overreacted after all. Maybe this was the fresh start I had been searching for, the peace I needed to leave my past behind. The darkness was gone now. I could feel it.

I rolled out of bed, the floorboards cool under my feet as I headed downstairs. For the first time since arriving, I wasn't bracing myself for anything—no shadows lurking in the corners, no strange whispers in the walls. Just me, in this moment, feeling like I could finally breathe again.

The kitchen was bathed in soft morning light, the kind that made everything feel new. I poured myself a cup of coffee, savoring the warmth, the quiet, the sense of calm that had been so elusive since I arrived. The weight that had clung to me for the last few days seemed to lift. I could finally enjoy something as simple as a cup of coffee without that creeping sense of unease gnawing at the back of my mind.

But then my cell phone rang, the shrill sound cutting through the stillness. My stomach sank as I glanced at the screen, the name flashing like a warning.

Trevor (my ex-boyfriend).

I froze. For a long moment, I stared at the phone, debating whether to answer. The urge to ignore it, to let it go to voicemail, was almost overpowering. But there was something in me, some twisted need to confront him, that made my finger swipe the screen before I could stop myself.

"Hello?" My voice was steadier than I felt, but my heart was already pounding, the memories of his voice and his fists flooding back in an instant.

There was silence on the other end for a beat, a silence that stretched out just long enough to make my skin crawl. And then his voice—low, cold, and laced with venom. "Izzy. You didn't think you could run forever, did you?"

A chill crawled up my spine, the peace from earlier evaporating in an instant. The sound of his voice was like a knife to the gut, sharp and cutting. "Trevor, I—"

"Shut up!" The words hit me like a slap. "You think you can just leave me? After everything we've been through? You're worthless without me, Izzy. You always were."

I could feel the old fear rising in me, the same fear that had kept me trapped for so long. But I wasn't that woman anymore. I hung up before he could say anything else, my hands trembling as I set the phone down on the counter. My heart hammered in my chest, and the memories came flooding back—every insult, every bruise, every time he made me feel like I was nothing.

I had left him. I had run from New Orleans to escape him, to get away from the man who had nearly broken me. But even now, miles away, he still had a hold on me. His voice was like poison, seeping into my thoughts, reminding me of all the things I was trying to forget.

I stood there for a long moment, gripping the counter until my knuckles turned white, trying to steady my breath.

I'm not that woman anymore. I'm free.

But the tension in my body refused to release, the weight of his words clinging to me like a shadow. I took a deep breath and tried to shake it off. As I turned to grab my coffee, a knock at the door jolted me out of my thoughts. I jumped, my pulse racing again, but this time, it wasn't fear that filled me.

I knew who it was before I even opened the door.

Billy.

He stood there, looking every bit as perfect as he had the day before. The sun hit his dark hair just right, making his eyes gleam like something out of a dream. His smile was enough to push Trevor's voice out of my head, at least for a little while.

"Hey, sleepyhead," he teased, leaning against the doorframe with that casual confidence that made my knees weak. "Thought you might want some company today."

I laughed, the tension from earlier beginning to unravel. "What did you have in mind?"

His eyes sparkled as he stepped closer, the space between us shrinking until I could feel the warmth radiating from him. "How about a day at the lake? It's beautiful out there today, and I thought you could use a little fun."

I hesitated for a second. My heart was still racing from the call, the anxiety still lingering in my chest, but Billy... Billy had a way of making everything else fade. When I was with him, the world felt simpler. Less dangerous. And right now, I needed that more than anything.

"I'd love to," I said, smiling despite myself.

Billy grinned, his eyes trailing over me in a way that made my skin tingle. "Great. I'll grab my stuff. Meet me outside in ten?"

"Deal," I replied, and with that, he was gone, leaving me standing there with my pulse racing for an entirely different reason.

The lake was breathtaking. The water shimmered under the afternoon sun, the trees swaying gently in the breeze. For the first time in days, I felt a sense of normalcy, like maybe, just maybe, I could start over here.

I had brought a picnic, and we spent the afternoon talking and laughing. Billy made me feel safe, like I wasn't alone in this strange, haunting place. But there were moments—small, fleeting moments—where I caught something in his eyes, something distant, like he was holding something back.

I noticed it most when I asked about his family. Every time I brought it up, even in passing, his expression would shift, his smile becoming a little too tight, his eyes darkening just enough to make me wonder. But then he would change the subject, effortlessly pulling me back into the moment, making me forget my questions. Still, I couldn't shake the feeling that there was something he wasn't telling me.

As the sun began to set, casting golden hues across the lake, we sat by the water, watching the colors shift in the sky. I glanced over at Billy, the fading light catching his profile, and my breath hitched. He was so... beautiful. And in that moment, I felt something I hadn't felt in a long time—safe. Like maybe, for the first time in years, I wasn't completely alone.

Billy must have felt me staring because he turned to me with that easy smile of his. "What?" he asked, his voice soft, teasing.

I shrugged, my heart thudding in my chest. "Nothing. Just... I'm glad you're here."

His smile softened, and for a moment, there was something deeper in his eyes, something I couldn't quite place. "I'm glad I'm here too," he said, his voice barely above a whisper.

Before I could think, before I could stop myself, I leaned in, closing the distance between us. Our lips met, and the kiss was soft at first, tentative, but it quickly deepened, growing more intense. My skin tingled with electricity, and my mind went blank, completely lost in the sensation of him. It was like nothing else mattered, like the world had disappeared, leaving just the two of us.

When we finally pulled apart, my breath was shaky, my heart pounding in my ears. Billy looked at me, his dark eyes intense, unreadable for a moment, before that teasing grin returned.

"You're full of surprises, Izzy," he murmured, his hand brushing a strand of hair behind my ear.

I laughed, trying to calm the butterflies that were doing somersaults in my stomach. "I could say the same about you."

We packed up and made our way back to my place. When we reached my door, I offered to drive him home, but he refused, just like before.

"Nah," he said, shaking his head. "I like walking. Gives me time to think."

I nodded, though something about it still felt... off.

Billy walked me to my door, and before I could say goodnight, he pulled me into his arms, holding me tight. His warmth enveloped me, and for a second, I felt like I could melt into him. He leaned down, kissing me again—slower this time, softer, but just as intense.

When he finally pulled back, his voice was low, almost a whisper. "I've been waiting a long time for someone like you, Izzy."

My heart skipped a beat, and I stared up at him, my mind spinning. "Billy..."

"I love you," he said softly, the words sending a shiver down my spine.

And then, just like that, he was gone, walking off into the night, leaving me standing at my door with my head spinning and my heart racing.

I closed the door behind me, leaning against it, trying to make sense of everything. What had just happened? How could I be feeling so much, so fast?

But even as the excitement and confusion swirled in my mind, there was something else creeping in. Something darker. Something I couldn't quite shake.

Who *was* Billy, really?

~ 8 ~

THE CAMEO

I woke up the next morning with that unsettling feeling again, like someone was watching me. I wasn't sure if it was the dream I had—a jumbled mess of forgotten faces and whispered warnings—or if it was something else. I rolled over in bed and glanced toward the window. The sun was shining brightly, casting a warm glow across the yard, but the brightness didn't ease my tension. Something was wrong. I could feel it. A gnawing unease, crawling under my skin.

"Stop being silly," I muttered to myself, trying to shake the feeling as I threw the covers off. Still, the sense of being watched clung to me like a second skin.

As I walked across the hardwood floor, my bare feet cold against the old planks, I noticed the door to the bedroom at the end of the hall. It was slightly ajar, though I was certain I had closed it the night before. My pulse quickened as I stood there, staring at the darkened gap.

For a split second, I swore I saw movement—a shadow or figure slipping out of view.

"Hello?" My voice wavered, barely louder than a whisper. My throat tightened as the silence settled back in, heavier than before. I stood frozen, heart pounding in my chest, waiting for a reply that never came. The house creaked, as old houses do, but the sound now felt deliberate, like it was answering me.

I swallowed hard, forcing myself to walk down the hall. My hand hesitated at the doorframe before pushing the door open fully. The bedroom was empty. Of course, it was. I exhaled a shaky breath, feeling ridiculous for even entertaining the idea that someone could be here. But just as I turned to leave, something caught my eye.

There, on the vanity, was a necklace. A beautiful, intricate cameo necklace, gold filigree, the face carved from shell and adorned with tiny rubies and diamonds. I knew it hadn't been there. I had been in this room the day before and hadn't seen it.

"This can't be real," I whispered, stepping closer. My fingers trembled as I reached out and touched the necklace, expecting it to dissolve into thin air. But it didn't. It was solid, tangible, and cool to the touch.

For a moment, I stood there, mesmerized by its beauty. I had seen cameos like this in antique shops, but this one seemed... different. There was something about the way the delicate face seemed to stare back at me, almost lifelike. I shook my head, breaking the spell, and carried it downstairs with me, feeling a strange compulsion to keep it close.

In the kitchen, I set the necklace down on the counter and poured myself a cup of coffee, trying to shake the unnerving feeling that had clung to me all morning. As the bitter warmth spread through me, I picked up the necklace again, examining it more closely. Who had left it? And why? I turned it over, half-expecting to find an inscription, but there was nothing. Just smooth, polished gold.

Before I could dwell on it further, my phone rang, making me jump. I grabbed it from the counter, relieved to see Donna's name flashing on the screen.

"Izzy, are you okay?" Donna's voice was rushed, her usual cheery tone replaced with something far more serious.

"Yeah, I'm fine. Why?" I asked, though my heart was racing again.

"I think Trevor is heading to Bayou Vista," she blurted. "I heard from a friend that he's been asking around about you."

My heart sank at the mention of Trevor. Of course, he'd come after me. That was just like him—always hovering like a dark cloud, waiting to strike. I hadn't told anyone the real reason I left New Orleans, not even Donna, though she knew enough to worry. But how could I explain it? How do I tell anyone that he threatened to kill me? That the man I once trusted had turned into something unrecognizable, dangerous?

"He called me yesterday," I said. "I knew he was looking for me, but how did he find out about Bayou Vista?"

"I think your Uncle James let it slip," she said. "That jerk knew he'd get it out of him."

"What should I do?" I asked quietly, glancing out the window, half-expecting to see Trevor there.

"Get out of the marsh," she urged. "Go into town, be around people. He won't try anything with witnesses."

I nodded, even though she couldn't see me. It was good advice. It was better to be around others than alone in this creaky old house in the middle of nowhere.

I threw on some clothes and grabbed my keys. After a moment's hesitation, I placed the necklace around my neck, the cool metal resting against my skin. For reasons I couldn't quite explain, I felt like it would protect me. Maybe it was silly, but part of me believed it might.

I drove into town, my eyes scanning every street and alley for Trevor's face. I pulled into the parking lot of *C&D Kwik Stop*, a small convenience store at the edge of town. As I walked in, the cool blast of air conditioning greeted me. Behind the counter stood a woman with blonde hair and a friendly smile. Next to her was a man wiping down the counter.

"Hey there," the woman said, looking up from the register. "Don't think I've seen you around here before. I'm Cindy, and this is my husband, Dondi."

I smiled nervously, feeling a little out of place. "I just moved to Bayou Vista. I'm Izzy."

"Well, welcome, Izzy! What brings you to this little slice of nowhere?" Dondi asked, eyeing me with curiosity.

I shrugged, trying to play it off. "Just needed a change, I guess. Quiet town, good place to start over."

Cindy raised an eyebrow. "Starting over, huh? Well, it's not as quiet as it seems."

I forced a laugh, even though her words sent a chill down my spine. "I'm starting to realize that."

We made small talk as I grabbed a few snacks for later. Just as I was about to leave, Preacher John came in, offering me a smile.

"Izzy," he said warmly. "Is everything okay with the house? You settling in alright?"

I nodded. "Yeah, just... getting used to the quiet."

"Thank goodness," he replied, though concern flickered in his eyes. "If you ever need anything, don't hesitate to ask."

I thanked him and hurried out, but the tension in my chest still hadn't eased. I needed to kill more time, to be around people, to distract myself from the gnawing unease that clung to me. So, I headed to *Frog's Delight*.

Frog's Delight was warm and smelled like sugar and cinnamon, a small comfort amid my growing anxiety. Behind the counter stood two women, chatting and laughing.

"Hi there!" one of the women greeted me. "I'm LaDonna, and this is Evelyn. You must be new in town."

I nodded. "Yeah, I'm Izzy."

"Well, welcome to Bayou Vista!" LaDonna said brightly. "We don't get too many newcomers, but we've got plenty of sweets to make you feel right at home."

"Thanks," I said, glancing around. "I was hoping to pick up a cake, you know, just in case I have company."

"Well, you came to the right place," Evelyn said. "We've got the best cakes in town."

As they boxed up my order, I felt a little more at ease. Truthfully, I was hoping Billy might stop by. I didn't want to be alone, especially not after hearing the news about Trevor. Maybe I was overthinking things. Maybe Trevor wouldn't show up. But just as I was about to leave, a low, rumbling truck engine echoed outside.

I froze, my stomach twisting. Trevor. It had to be him. I rushed to the window, but there was no truck in sight. My heart pounded in my ears as I turned back to the counter.

"Everything alright, dear?" LaDonna asked.

I forced a smile. "Yeah, just... jumpy, I guess."

After leaving the bakery, I went straight to the Sheriff's office. Better to be safe. The Sheriff listened as I explained my concerns about Trevor, nodding as if he'd heard this story a thousand times before.

"You let me know if he shows up," he said, though there was something in his tone that suggested he wasn't taking me seriously.

I nodded, thanked him, and left. As I stepped outside, I found myself drawn to *Micky's Magical Things*, the shop I'd heard so much about. Feeling compelled to see it for myself, I walked in. The air inside hummed with a soft, mystical energy, and the shelves were filled with an intriguing assortment of objects. Micky stood near the counter, quietly talking to a woman who was wiping away tears.

"Thank you, Micky, for the message from my son," she said, her voice thick with emotion, before she left the shop.

Micky turned his attention to me, smiling warmly. "Well, hello, Izzy. I was wondering when you'd stop by."

I blinked in surprise. "How do you know my name?"

He chuckled softly. "Everybody's talking about the lady with the red Corvette who bought the house in Devil's Marsh."

His eyes drifted to the cameo necklace I was wearing, and I noticed his expression change—his eyes widening in recognition. Instinctively, I buttoned my blouse higher, hiding the cameo from view.

"Anything strange out there?" he asked, his voice calm but curious.

I hesitated. "Well, there were a few things, but Preacher John came out and blessed the house. It stopped after that."

Micky nodded slowly. "If you ever need anything, or just want to talk, you know where to find me."

"Thanks," I replied, starting to leave.

Just as I turned to go, Micky's tone grew more serious. "Your mom and dad are with you, Izzy, and they want you to leave that house. You're in danger."

My heart skipped a beat. I spun back toward him, my voice tight with disbelief. "How did you know about my mom and dad?"

He gave me a gentle smile, his eyes soft yet piercing. "Your mom wants to know what happened to the ruby ring she gave you."

My breath hitched, and a knot of dread tightened in my stomach. How did he know about the ruby ring? Trevor had stolen that ring from me and pawned it a couple of years ago. I couldn't respond, couldn't explain. With a hurried nod, I thanked him and left the shop, feeling more unsettled than ever.

I drove home with my hands gripping the steering wheel so tightly my knuckles turned white. The whole way, I kept glancing in the rearview mirror, half-expecting to see Trevor following me. But the road was empty.

When I got back to the house, the uneasy feeling returned. I couldn't shake the sense that something was wrong, that someone—something—was watching me. I explored more of the rooms, trying to distract myself, but instead, I found something far worse.

In one of the untouched rooms, I found a nursery. The room was old, untouched for years by the looks of it, but there was a strange energy to it. The faded wallpaper, once cheerful, now seemed cold and distant. There was something unsettling about this space, as if it held memories best forgotten. The crib, sitting in the corner, caught my eye. It didn't fit with the rest of the house, almost as if it had been left behind on purpose. A wave of discomfort washed over me, and I hesitated before stepping closer. My chest tightened as I ran my fingers along the faded wood, feeling an eerie chill creep up my spine. Why would there be a nursery in a house like this? Who lived here before? What had happened to them?

I shivered, the room suddenly feeling colder. A soft creak behind me made me whirl around, but there was nothing there. The house was still, yet it felt alive—watching, waiting.

Trying to shake the feeling, I walked to the window, staring out into the yard. The last thing I wanted was to be stuck inside with my thoughts spiraling out of control. I was about to turn away when I saw him.

A clown.

He stood at the edge of the property, his face painted white with a blood-red smile. My heart stopped, every muscle in my body freezing as a cold terror gripped me. I blinked, hoping it was just a trick of the light, but when I looked again, the clown was still there. His painted eyes seemed to lock onto mine, his smile unnaturally wide. I could feel my pulse in my ears, a rush of fear that turned my legs to lead.

I couldn't move.

A scream clawed at my throat, but it wouldn't come out. My mouth was dry, my hands trembling as I stood there, paralyzed with fear. *What is this?* I thought. *Who—what—is that?*

I blinked again, and the clown was gone. In his place stood Trevor.

No. This wasn't possible. Trevor couldn't be here. Not already. Not now. *Had he been the clown?* I didn't know what was worse—Trevor or the possibility that my mind was playing tricks on me. I stumbled backward, my pulse racing, a cold sweat breaking out along my skin. The necklace around my neck suddenly felt heavy, burning against my chest.

I ripped it off, throwing it to the floor as the cold air seemed to thicken around me. The house, once just old and creaky, now felt suffocating, like it was closing in on me. I couldn't breathe. I had to get out.

I stumbled back from the window, my heart hammering in my chest, my pulse deafening in my ears. Panic surged through me as I fumbled for my phone, my hands trembling. I rushed downstairs, barely able to dial the Sheriff's number.

"Sheriff... Sheriff Johnson, it's Izzy. Trevor—he's here. I saw him," I said breathlessly, my voice shaky, almost breaking.

There was a pause on the other end, longer than I expected. "I'll be right over," he said, but there was something in his voice that felt off—like he was reluctant.

By the time the cruiser pulled up, Trevor was already long gone.

Sheriff Johnson stepped out, his eyes scanning the house, his posture tense. He didn't even bother with the usual polite nod as he approached, instead casting quick glances around, like something might jump out at any second.

"Izzy, are you sure you saw him?" he asked, his voice low, but there was something else there—something that didn't sit right.

"I'm sure," I whispered, wrapping my arms around myself. I pointed toward the window. "He was right there, Sheriff. Watching me."

The Sheriff rubbed the back of his neck, a deep frown crossing his face as he glanced at the yard. "You didn't see any... anyone else?" His eyes flickered toward me, uneasy.

I hesitated, my mouth dry. *The clown... I wanted to tell him, but how could I? He'd think I was losing it.* Instead, I shook my head. "No, just Trevor."

Sheriff Johnson shifted uncomfortably, glancing back toward his car, like he didn't want to be here. "I haven't been out here in a long time... since the last people who lived here." His voice trailed off, and he swallowed hard before continuing. "They disappeared two years ago. No one's seen or heard from them since."

I blinked, the words hitting me like a punch to the gut. "What do you mean, disappeared?"

"They were a quiet couple, Don and Anna, from Michigan," he said, glancing around again. "Good folks, didn't cause any trouble, but then one day... gone. No trace. People assumed they got scared and headed back up north, but..." He shook his head, his voice lowering. "Nobody knows for sure what happened. This place has quite a reputation."

I stared at him, feeling the blood drain from my face. *Anna... that's the journal I found.* My heart raced as the pieces started clicking together. Could it be the same Anna? The quiet woman who once lived here, whose words were now trapped in those tattered pages? I swallowed hard, my mind swirling with questions. What happened to them? Why was her journal left behind, abandoned like the life they seemed to have vanished from?

The Sheriff shifted his weight again, his fingers tapping nervously against his belt. "I don't like being out here," he admitted, almost like he was talking to himself. "There's something... off about this place."

I could feel it too. The air was thick, oppressive. It pressed down on me, making it hard to breathe. The walls felt like they were closing in once again, like the house itself was listening.

"What do I do?" I asked, my voice small, barely a whisper. Fear tightened its grip on me.

Sheriff Johnson sighed, looking at me with pity in his eyes. "I'll keep an eye on the area, but Izzy... you might want to consider staying somewhere else for a while. Just until things settle down. At least until Trevor is found," His gaze lingered on the house behind me, uneasy, like he could feel the weight of its secrets too.

"I can't leave," I whispered, more to myself than to him. But the words felt hollow, like a lie.

He nodded slowly. "If anything else happens, you call me. Don't hesitate."

As he walked back to his car, I stood there, frozen in place, watching him go. The silence that followed was deafening, and the weight of his words settled over me like a heavy fog. Inside my head, a voice screamed, *Don't leave me alone.* But no sound escaped my lips, and I just stood there, paralyzed by fear.

Night came quickly, and with it, a thick blanket of fear. Every creak, every whisper of wind seemed like a warning. I locked every door, pulled the curtains shut, but it didn't feel like enough. The house felt alive, watching me, waiting for something.

For hours, I sat in the kitchen, hands trembling around a hot cup of tea, trying to steady myself. *This is ridiculous,* I thought. *You need to get some sleep.* But the unease wouldn't leave me. My mind kept drifting back to the nursery, as if it was pulling at me, demanding attention.

I couldn't shake the feeling that something was deeply wrong in that room, as if it held memories too dark to surface—memories that shouldn't be remembered.

And then, a knock at the door.

I froze, the warmth of the tea slipping away as my skin prickled. The clock on the wall caught my eye. **3:33**.

I froze, the sound reverberating through the silent house. My heart pounded in my chest. I didn't move. I couldn't.

The knock came again, harder this time.

I backed away from the door, my breath coming in shallow gasps. *Who could be out there? Trevor? Or worse...?* I couldn't face whatever was out there. Not tonight.

Without thinking, I ran up the stairs and into the nursery. The room felt frigid, as if the warmth had been drained from it, but I didn't care. I crawled into the corner, my knees tucked up to my chest, trembling.

I listened, every fiber of my being on edge, waiting for the next knock.

But all I heard was the sound of my own heartbeat, hammering in the silence.

THE HAUNTING
FOOTPRINTS

I jolted awake, my heart racing. My eyes flew open, and I froze. The air felt thick, heavy with an oppressive, suffocating stillness. The room around me was unfamiliar, but I knew where I was—the nursery.

My chest tightened as I glanced around, the room dimly lit by the pale gray light of early morning. The crib, draped in cobwebs, stood in the corner like a forgotten relic. A small rocking chair creaked slightly, though there was no breeze. Old, worn toys littered the floor, as if waiting for children who never returned.Top of FormBottom of Form

I swallowed hard, trying to keep my panic from spiraling. The nursery had unsettled me from the moment I first found it, and now, here I was, waking up inside it, as if I'd been drawn there. What was happening to me?

My eyes landed on the floor, where the cameo necklace I'd found yesterday lay, its chain twisted. My breath caught in my throat as I snatched it up, the cool metal sending a chill through my fingers. I looked out the window and froze.

Footprints. Right where I'd seen Trevor and that clown.

My stomach lurched. I stumbled backward, clutching the cameo to my chest as my mind raced. The image of Trevor, standing with that painted face, twisted my gut. Could it really have been him? It had to be. That meant he'd been here, outside the house, watching me. And now his footprints were staring back at me, haunting reminders that he'd gotten closer than I ever thought possible.

Then it hit me like a punch to the gut—the clown could have been Trevor all along. He's always been good at digging into the dark corners of people's pasts, researching places like it was second nature to him. He must've stumbled across the story of the man who murdered his family with his face painted like a clown, and Trevor being Trevor, twisted it into his own sick game. He knew exactly how to get under my skin. He always loved to frighten me, to see that look of terror in my eyes. Maybe this was his latest way of trying to control me, using the fear that still haunted me to remind me that he was always there, lurking in the shadows, watching.

I had to call the Sheriff. There was no other choice.

Sheriff Johnson showed up faster than I expected, with two deputies in tow. They spread out across the yard, checking every inch, while I stood on the porch, hugging myself, trying to make sense of it all. I couldn't take my eyes off those footprints—they were still so fresh, like they had just been made.

"You okay, Izzy?" Sheriff Johnson asked as he approached, his face serious.

I nodded, though I wasn't sure if I was. *It was Trevor, wasn't it? I saw him... or maybe I saw that clown, but I think it was him.*

The Sheriff's brow furrowed. "We'll find out what's going on, but you need to stay calm, alright? We'll search the area."

I watched as they moved through the yard, calling out to each other as they followed the footprints that led toward the swamp. The murky waters of Devil's Marsh loomed in the distance, thick and still. I couldn't help but feel a pull toward it, like it was hiding something—something dark.

Hours passed, and the sun climbed higher in the sky, but still no sign of Trevor. Then, just after noon, one of the deputies radioed in. "We found something in the swamp," he said, his voice crackling over the speaker. "It's a truck."

My breath caught—Trevor's truck.

I followed the Sheriff and his deputies down to the edge of the marsh. There it was, half-submerged in the murky water, almost hidden by the thick brush. My heart pounded as I stared at it, the realization sinking in. Trevor had been here, alright—closer than I ever wanted him to be.

The Sheriff sighed, narrowing his eyes. "Is this Trevor's truck?"

I nodded, swallowing hard. "It is."

He bent down, peering at the vehicle as it sat partially buried in the water. "Probably drove straight into the marsh."

"And Trevor?" I asked, though I already knew the answer.

The Sheriff straightened up, looking out toward the still water. "There's a lot of gators in that marsh," he said quietly. "If he went in there, he's not coming back out."

I wasn't sure how to feel. Relief flooded through me in one sense—Trevor was gone. He couldn't hurt me anymore. But there was also a gnawing sense of dread, a fear that I'd never really escape him, not even in death. And that clown... what if it hadn't been Trevor at all? What if something else was lurking in Devil's Marsh?

The Sheriff patted my shoulder, bringing me back to the moment. "Let's head back to town. We'll file the report, and you can put this behind you."

I nodded and turned back toward the house, quickly grabbing my purse and locking the door behind me before heading to the car. My thoughts were spinning as I started the engine and followed the Sheriff out of the driveway, keeping close behind him. The slow drive back to town felt endless, each passing mile doing little to settle the growing knot in my stomach. I kept my eyes on the Sheriff's truck ahead, but my mind wandered back to the marsh, to Trevor's truck submerged in that murky water.

By the time we reached the Sheriff's office, the unease had settled deep in my bones. I parked and sat for a moment, gripping the steering wheel tightly as the weight of it all sank in. Something about this didn't sit right with me. The whole drive, I kept trying to piece things together, but nothing fit.

I stepped out of the car, glancing at the dark clouds gathering on the horizon. The storm was coming, but I couldn't shake the feeling that something far worse had already arrived.

Once the formalities were done, I left the office feeling drained, the weight of everything pressing down on me. I didn't want to go back to the house, not yet. So, instead, I stopped by *Jason's Bar*, hoping a drink might calm my nerves.

Jason's Bar was quiet, a few locals scattered at the tables, nursing their beers. I took a seat at the bar, the familiar buzz of small-town chatter easing the tension in my chest.

The gruff-looking man behind the bar gave me a nod as I slid onto the stool. His weathered face softened with a friendly smile. "New in town, right?" he asked, his voice warm despite his rough exterior.

I nodded. "Yeah, just moved here."

He wiped down the counter before extending a hand. "Name's Jason Riesenbeck. I own the place."

"My name is Izzy," I said, offering a small smile.

"Nice to meet you, Izzy," he said, sliding a glass of whiskey my way. "First drink's on me. Welcome to Bayou Vista."

I thanked him and took a sip, the burn of the alcohol warming my throat. Just as I was starting to relax, I heard a familiar voice behind me.

"Well, look who it is," Shanster grinned as she slid onto the stool next to me. "You adjusting to our little town yet?"

I laughed, though it felt forced. "I'm getting there."

Shanster raised an eyebrow, sensing my unease. "You okay? You look like you've seen a ghost."

"Something like that," I muttered, taking another sip of my drink. "It's just been a weird day."

She nodded, her expression softening. "Yeah, this place can do that to you. Devil's Marsh has a way of getting under your skin."

I glanced at her, wondering how much she knew. "You ever hear any stories about the house? The one I'm living in?"

Shanster's grin faded, her eyes darkening. "More than I'd care to admit. But that's Bayou Vista for you. It's full of stories... some of them better left untold."

Her words sent a chill down my spine, but before I could ask more, Jason came over to refill our drinks. Shanster gave me a quick wink, changing the subject to something lighter, and we spent the next half hour chatting about small-town life, local gossip, and the best places to visit around town. Her energy was contagious, and for the first time all day, I felt a bit more grounded.

After leaving the Sheriff's office, I decided to swing by *Tanya's Crawfish Shack* to grab dinner. The thought of going back to that empty house without some sort of distraction was too much to bear.

Tanya greeted me with a warm smile. "What can I get for you, Izzy?"

"Just something for dinner," I replied. "I'm thinking a crawfish platter."

"You got it," she said, motioning for me to follow her. She led me to a booth near the window, and I slid into the seat as she handed me a glass of water. "How's the house treating you?"

I hesitated, not sure how much to share. "It's... interesting. Definitely a lot to get used to."

Tanya chuckled, shaking her head as she stood by the booth. "That's Devil's Marsh for you. It's got a way of keeping you on your toes."

Just as I settled into the booth to wait for my order, Gail, Patricia, and another woman walked in. Their eyes quickly spotted me, and they headed over with warm smiles. The unfamiliar woman, with a bright smile, waved as they made their way over.

"Mind if we join you?" Gail asked, sliding into the seat across from me.

"Of course," I replied, glancing at the woman I didn't recognize.

Gail gestured toward her. "This is Tina Kazee. She runs *Bayou Belle Beauty* here in town."

Tina leaned forward, her eyes lighting up. "Nice to meet you, Izzy! You should come in tomorrow and let me take care of you. We could get you settled in with a fresh style."

"I'd love that," I said with a smile. "I'll definitely stop by."

The conversation shifted as they asked how I was adjusting to the house. Patricia arched an eyebrow, her voice teasing. "Have you seen anything strange around that place yet?"

I shifted uncomfortably, debating whether to mention it. "Not much... but I did meet Micky. That man gives me the creeps," I admitted, my voice dropping slightly.

Gail chuckled softly and shook her head. "Oh, honey, Micky's nothing to be scared of. He's just... different. He knows things—things most of us can't even comprehend. People travel from miles away just to see him. He talks to spirits, helps the police solve cases, and even performs exorcisms. He's a minister too, but more than that—he's become a legend in this town.

As Gail spoke, my intrigue deepened. Micky's reputation was clearly much larger than I'd realized, but despite the town's trust in him, something about him still made my skin crawl.

Gail noticed my hesitation. "Did he tell you something that rattled you?"

I sighed and nodded. "Yes, he did."

A sly smile tugged at Gail's lips. "That's Micky for you. He doesn't sugarcoat anything. But don't let it get to you—he always knows more than he lets on, and trust me, he's got this town's best interests at heart."

After finishing dinner and saying goodbye to the women, I hurried to my car, trying to shake the unease that clung to me. The rain pounded down, drumming against the roof as I started the engine. The sky had darkened, with storm clouds looming overhead. As I drove back toward Devil's Marsh, the relentless rain couldn't drown out the thoughts swirling in my mind. Gail's words about Micky echoed over and over.

What if she was right? What if Micky knew far more than he ever let on? He wasn't just some strange man. He could talk to spirits, solve crimes, even perform exorcisms. The thought gnawed at me, filling me with a deep sense of unease. How did he know about my mom's ring? The question lingered, wrapping itself around my thoughts like a dark cloud. Maybe I didn't want to know the answer.

I think I need to start going into town every day. I was used to seeing Donna daily—that's what helped me survive Trevor. I'd give anything to make a friend like her in Bayou Vista, and maybe getting to know Micky better would help me understand this place—and him.

The rain hammered against the car, each drop louder than the last, drowning out everything else. The isolation closed in, more palpable with each passing moment. My eyes caught movement—shadows flickering at the edges of my vision. I turned, heart pounding, but there was nothing. My breath quickened. Was it my imagination? Or was something really out there, watching me?

I shook my head, trying to dispel the unease, but the feeling wouldn't go away.

The headlights barely pierced through the downpour as I neared the house. Then, I saw it. My heart stopped. Someone was standing on the porch. Still. Tall. My pulse raced. For a second, I thought it was Billy. I wanted it to be Billy. But... it didn't move. It just stood there, shrouded in the rain and darkness, like a shadow that had come to life.

I leaned forward, trying to make sense of what I was seeing. The figure was just standing there, waiting. My throat tightened, panic rising in my chest. The rain twisted the image, but it stayed there. Unmoving. The closer I got, the more wrong it felt. Then—just like that—it disappeared. Gone. Swallowed by the storm, as if it was never there.

I gasped, gripping the steering wheel. Was it my imagination? Had I really seen someone? A shiver ran down my spine as I stared at the empty porch. The rain pounded harder, each drop echoing the fear building inside me. The shadows outside seemed darker, more alive. Something was watching me. I could feel it.

Billy said he loved me—so where was he? Why hadn't he come back? The questions spun in my mind, feeding the fear. What if that wasn't Billy? What if it was something else? Something worse? Trevor?

I forced myself out of the car, rain drenching me instantly, soaking through my clothes. My heart pounded in my chest as I ran toward the house, each step feeling heavier, slower than the last. The air was thick, almost suffocating. I looked at the porch again, my eyes darting from shadow to shadow. Nothing. Just emptiness.

But the unease lingered, gripping me tighter with each passing second. I swallowed hard, my breath shaky. Was it my mind playing tricks? Or had something—someone—been there?

I fumbled with my keys, my hands shaking. I glanced over my shoulder one last time, half-expecting that figure to return. But the porch stayed empty, still as death. I rushed inside, locking the door behind me. But even then, the feeling of safety didn't come.

The silence inside the house felt wrong. My wet clothes stuck to my skin, but I barely noticed. My nerves were shot. I could hear my pulse pounding in my ears, my eyes scanning the shadows. The room felt darker, the corners seemed to close in around me.

The storm outside raged on, but it was nothing compared to the storm inside my head. Thoughts of Billy twisted in my mind. Why had he left? Why wasn't he here? And that figure—was it him? Was it Trevor? Or was I losing my grip?

I swallowed, my throat tight. My hands shook as I stared out the window. The storm outside offered no answers, only darkness. And as the rain poured and the wind howled, the truth became clear.

I wasn't alone.

Then, just as I began to turn away from the window, there it was—a faint knock. So soft, it could have been the wind. I froze, my breath catching in my throat. Another knock, louder this time. My heart raced. I stood perfectly still, straining to hear over the storm.

A whisper drifted through the air, barely audible, but unmistakable—my name.

"Izzy..."

I backed away from the window, my skin crawling. My heart thundered in my chest as I stared into the darkened room, the shadows seeming to move. The house felt alive, watching me, waiting.

"Billy?" I whispered.

A cold chill ran down my spine as the whisper came again, closer this time.

"Izzy..."

Was it Billy? Or was my mind unraveling without him? Either way, the fear clawed deeper, and I wasn't sure I wanted to know the answer.

~ 10 ~

BEAUTY AND ROSES

I jolted awake on the couch, my heart hammering in my chest. The low hum of the TV barely registered over the pounding in my ears. My mind kept circling back to the knock on the door—the one I hadn't dared to answer. I had sat there, paralyzed, afraid to even breathe. Who had been there? The thought clawed at me relentlessly. What if it had been Trevor, standing on the other side, waiting? The fear, heavy and suffocating, wrapped itself tighter around me, squeezing the air from my lungs.

I stood slowly, muscles aching, as if the weight of my own fear had taken a physical toll. My damp clothes from yesterday clung uncomfortably to my skin, a reminder that I hadn't even bothered to change. Shivering, I rubbed my arms, feeling the morning air creep into the house, chilling me further. I needed to shake this off—whatever *this* was. I'd head into town today, distract myself. Maybe a little pampering at *Bayou Belle Beauty* would help settle my nerves.

After changing into fresh clothes, I stepped out onto the porch, ready to leave the strange tension behind. And then I froze.

There he was—Billy. He leaned casually against the porch railing, his hands tucked in his pockets, like he had all the time in the world. A slow, crooked smile spread across his face as his eyes met mine, and suddenly, my heart wasn't pounding from fear anymore.

"Morning, beautiful," he drawled, that grin deepening as his eyes crinkled at the corners.

I blinked, startled but oddly pleased to see him. "Billy! Where've you been? You disappeared on me." I crossed my arms, pretending to be annoyed, but the way my heart skipped told a different story.

He stepped closer, his gaze never leaving mine. "I did stop by, Izzy. A few times, actually. You never answered the door." His voice was smooth, teasing.

I felt a blush creep up my neck. *Of course, I hadn't answered. I was too scared, hiding under blankets like a child.* "Maybe I didn't hear you," I said, knowing full well that wasn't true.

Billy chuckled softly, the sound rumbling deep in his chest. He leaned in, just enough for me to catch the scent of him—earthy, masculine, like pine trees after rain. "Or maybe you were avoiding me," he teased, his breath warm against my ear.

I swatted at him, laughing, trying to hide how flustered I felt. "Trust me, Billy, if I was avoiding you, you'd know."

He raised an eyebrow, that grin widening. "Oh, I don't know, Izzy. You seem like the kind of girl who likes to keep a man guessing."

I rolled my eyes, trying to play it cool. "Maybe I do. But you seem like the kind of guy who doesn't give up easily."

Billy chuckled again, stepping back just enough to give me space to breathe. "You're right about that, sweetheart. I'll be around tomorrow—maybe you'll answer the door this time," he teased, his eyes glinting with mischief. He paused for a moment, his gaze lingering on mine. "I have a surprise for you," he added, his voice dipping into something darker, more playful. Then, with a wink, he turned to leave, his movements easy, fluid, like he owned every space he walked into.

I stood there for a moment, watching him go, feeling a strange mix of excitement and nervousness. Billy had a way of getting under my skin, in a good way. I shook my head, laughing at myself, and grabbed my keys.

As I got into my car and pulled down the driveway, I glanced in the direction Billy had gone, expecting to see him walking away. But he wasn't there. The road was empty, flanked by thick trees and patches of marsh where dark water pooled along the edges. I slowed down, scanning the stretch of dirt and mist rising off the ground. Where had he gone? There were no side paths or shortcuts that I could see—he had vanished, like he was never there. A chill ran through me, but I pushed it aside.

Maybe he knew a back way through the woods, or perhaps I'd just missed him turning a corner.

Shaking off the unease, I turned onto the main road. The trees thinned as marshland stretched out, the damp air heavy with the scent of wet earth and decay. Dark water still pooled in the low spots along the road, and even inside the car, the soft rustling of leaves reached my ears, something unseen moving through the brush.

My thoughts kept drifting back to Billy—his playful smile, his teasing words. It felt good, exciting, like I was stepping into something new, even if I wasn't sure what that "*something*" was yet.

By the time I reached *Bayou Belle Beauty*, I was more than ready for a change of scenery. The salon was buzzing when I arrived. It wasn't just a place for haircuts and highlights—it was the town's gossip mill, and everyone seemed to be in on the latest whispers. The second I walked in, the noise hit me—laughter, chatter, the hum of blow dryers. It was like stepping into a different world.

Tina spotted me from across the room and waved me over. "Izzy! Girl, come on in! We've been waiting for you."

I smiled and made my way over to her station. "Seems like a busy day."

"You have no idea," Tina said with a laugh, patting the chair. "Sit down, honey. We're gonna get you all fixed up. I'll highlight your beautiful auburn hair with a few golden streaks—it'll really make it pop!"

As I settled in, a few other women started looking my way. Tina introduced them one by one. "This here's Mary

Balow," she said, pointing to a woman with short, wavy, dark hair and sharp eyes. "She's our other stylist."

Mary nodded at me, her smile polite but curious. "Nice to meet you, Izzy. We've heard a bit about you."

I raised an eyebrow. "All good things, I hope?"

"Mostly," Mary said with a wink.

Next, Tina motioned to a girl across the room. "That's Stephanie Terry. She's Gail's daughter and does nails part-time."

Stephanie looked up and waved with a warm smile. "Hi, Izzy! Glad you stopped by."

Then Tina introduced me to the other women sitting in various chairs, each one chipping in their own little greeting.

"Matilda Shabino—she drives the school bus," Tina said, pointing to a woman with a stern face, though it softened with a big smile as she nodded at me. "And Jill Ecker, Loretta's friend. You'll be seeing a lot of her."

Jill smiled shyly, her blonde hair tied up in a messy bun. "Hey, nice to meet you."

"Tricia Grigar—Loretta's other friend," Tina added, as Tricia, a woman with red hair, waved. "She's our resident celebrity. You've probably heard about her books."

"Books?" I asked, intrigued.

"Oh yeah," Tricia said, her voice smooth and confident. "I write thrillers. My latest series is about that serial killer here in Bayou Vista. You know, the one they never caught."

The other women leaned in closer, the air thick with gossip.

"You should see the men in this town act," Matilda piped in. "Like Brock Whitmore, all holier-than-thou, and yet we all know he's gambling and cheating on his wife."

Mary laughed sharply. "Oh, don't get me started on Brock. Pretending like he's the town's moral compass. Ha!"

The conversation quickly spiraled into more gossip about Brock, about men in town who couldn't keep their hands to themselves or their money out of the casino. I listened, fascinated.

"So, Izzy," Stephanie said, turning to me with a sly grin. "Got yourself a boyfriend?"

I blushed, a little caught off guard. "Well, there's this guy...Billy. We've been seeing each other."

"Ooh, Billy," Tricia teased, raising her eyebrows. "Tell us more."

I smiled, feeling a little giddy talking about him. "He's...different. Mysterious. He's kind of...always there when I need him."

"Sounds like a keeper," Mary said, giving me a wink. "Just be careful with those mysterious types, though."

"I'm always careful," I said with a laugh, though part of me wondered if I should be.

After my hair was done, highlighted and feeling fresh, I thanked Tina and promised I'd be back soon. The town may have its fair share of strange happenings, but these women were starting to feel like they could be part of my circle.

On my way home, I decided to stop by *Micky's Magical Things*. The door chimed as I stepped inside, and the familiar scent of herbs and old books wrapped around me. Micky looked up from behind the counter, his eyes twinkling.

"Izzy," he said warmly. "What brings you in today?"

I walked up to the counter, feeling a bit embarrassed. "I wanted to apologize. The other day... I wasn't myself. You scared me, but that wasn't your fault."

Micky waved his hand. "No need for apologies, dear. I'm just glad you're all right."

I paused for a moment, leaning in closer. "Micky... I've been seeing strange things since Preacher John came out to the house. Things I can't explain."

His expression darkened, and he leaned forward, too. "Strange how?"

I lowered my voice. "I think... I think it was Trevor, my ex-boyfriend. I saw something—or someone—watching me."

Micky's eyes narrowed. "Trevor... or something else?"

I shrugged, feeling a chill run down my spine. "I don't know. But it felt wrong, like the air was thick with it."

He nodded slowly, his expression unreadable. "Keep an eye out, Izzy. The Marsh... it holds old secrets, dark ones. And sometimes, they don't stay buried." He hesitated for a moment, his gaze searching mine. "Do you need my help?"

I shook my head, though uncertainty gnawed at me. "Not yet," I said softly, though part of me wondered if I should have asked for it right then. I swallowed, feeling my skin crawl. "Thanks, Micky. I'll be careful."

"Any time you need something," he said, his voice gentle but firm, "you come see me. I mean that."

I nodded, grateful for his kindness, though his words lingered, heavy and unsettling.

The drive home was quiet, but my mind raced. Every shadow stretched too far, every rustle in the trees sounded too loud, like the marsh itself was watching. By the time I pulled into the driveway, the unease had taken root deep inside me.

Then I saw them—a dozen white roses, neatly tied with a ribbon, sitting on my porch. My heart sank. Could they be from Billy? Or Trevor... he always gave me a dozen white roses after we fought.

My stomach twisted as I bent down, hands trembling, to pick up the card nestled in the bouquet.

The handwriting was jagged, almost frantic, as if written in haste or rage:

Roses are white, but blood is red. Soon, you'll see what's inside your head. The marsh calls to those who stray, Beware, Izzy, it's coming your way.

I dropped the card, my heart racing. The roses seemed to glow in the fading light, a stark contrast to the dark feeling that crept into my bones.

I left them there, not daring to bring them inside.

When I raced through the door, the air inside the house felt...wrong. Heavy. I turned toward the living room, and my breath caught in my throat.

The picture—the one of the woman with hollow eyes, the one I had taken down—it was back on the wall.

Watching. Waiting.

The silence pressed in around me, thick and suffocating. My pulse pounded in my ears as I backed away, my hands trembling.

I wasn't alone. And I wasn't safe.

Something, or someone, was watching me.

And they weren't done yet.

~ 11 ~

WHISPERS BENEATH THE SURFACE

I sat at the kitchen table, staring into my coffee. The rich, dark liquid swirled lazily, mirroring my thoughts. Last night, I had seen the roses. I had read that poem. But now, in the harsh morning light, I looked on the porch and they were gone—like they had never been there at all. Had it been a dream? A trick of my mind? Or was it something worse, something I wasn't ready to face?

My thoughts kept circling back to Trevor, the man I had buried in my mind the day I left New Orleans, yet here he was again, crawling out from the darkest corners of my memories. Could he still be alive? The idea gnawed at me like a parasite, pulling me back to those years—those suffocating years I had spent with him. He was cruel, manipulative, but resourceful. If anyone could make me feel haunted, even from beyond the grave, it was Trevor.

I took a long, bitter sip of coffee, trying to steady myself. If Trevor was alive, I needed to be prepared. If it wasn't Trevor... my stomach twisted. I didn't even want to think about the alternative.

A sudden knock at the door snapped me out of my thoughts, and the coffee cup clattered in its saucer. I wasn't ready for more surprises. Not yet.

Opening the door, I found Cindy Blevins standing there with her usual bright red lipstick and a strained, forced smile, as if trying too hard to mask the fear of coming out to the marsh. She clutched a gift basket wrapped in cellophane, but something about her looked... off. Her eyes flitted nervously around, like she couldn't stand still for long.

"Morning, Izzy," she said, her voice too cheery for the tension hanging in the air. "I thought you might like a little something from *Burning Love*—candles, bath salts, you know, just a welcome gift."

"Thank you, Cindy," I said, trying to sound as normal as possible, though my thoughts were still racing. As I took the basket, I glanced down at the porch again, where the roses had been last night. Not a single petal. Nothing. Like it had never happened at all. "Come in, if you'd like."

Cindy hesitated at the threshold, her smile faltering for just a second before she stepped inside. Her eyes flicked toward the walls, toward the bottom of the stairs, at the photograph of the hollow-eyed woman. She didn't say anything, but I could tell she was scanning the room, her eyes darting around like she was expecting something to leap out at her.

"You okay?" I asked, trying to keep my voice casual, but I could hear the unease creeping in.

"Yeah, yeah, just... a little chilly." She rubbed her arms, though the house wasn't cold at all. If anything, it felt stifling, like the air was too thick to breathe. She kept glancing around, her movements stiff, like she was trying to hide something.

"Can I get you some coffee?" I asked, though I could already see her discomfort. I had this creeping feeling she didn't want to be here, but I couldn't tell if it was because of me or... the house.

"No, thanks," she said, her voice quieter now, almost like she was speaking to someone else in the room. She shivered again, and I saw goosebumps rising on her skin. "Old houses... you know how they are," she added, but her forced smile betrayed her nerves.

I followed her gaze as it lingered on the ceiling, just for a moment. Then, she shifted, clearly wanting to leave. "I should go... I need to open the shop."

Her words felt like an excuse, a reason to flee, and I couldn't shake the feeling that she was hiding something. Before I could question her, she was already at the door, throwing a quick goodbye over her shoulder. "Be careful here... I mean, settle in, okay?"

And just like that, she was gone.

I closed the door, and suddenly, the house felt heavier, as if the very walls were closing in. I stood there for a moment, letting the silence swallow me whole. It was then that I heard it—the crash from the attic above, loud and sudden, like something heavy had fallen.

My pulse quickened. I couldn't ignore it.

Grabbing a flashlight, I forced myself up the stairs, each creak beneath my feet sending shivers up my spine. My mind raced. Maybe it was nothing. Maybe it was just the house settling, or perhaps the wind rattling through the old windows, making everything feel more eerie than it should.

But I knew better.

When I reached the attic door, I hesitated. My hand hovered over the knob, my heart pounding so hard I could feel it in my throat. Slowly, I pushed the door open, and the dim light from the small window at the far end cast long, ghostly shadows across the room.

I stepped inside, my flashlight sweeping the space. Dust particles hung in the air, and everything seemed still, untouched. I hesitated, then climbed the stairs, each creak echoing in the silence. But then I saw it, tucked away in the corner.

The photograph.

I swallowed hard and moved closer. It was different this time—a family portrait. My stomach knotted as I approached, my pulse hammering in my ears. The image was old, but one face stood out immediately.

Billy...

Or someone who looked just like him. Three men, the woman with hollow eyes, and a young girl holding a baby.

My fingers trembled as I flipped the photograph over. It was dated, December 1974.

My breath caught in my throat. *How? The man in the photograph—it was Billy. But this picture was from decades ago. That would make him... what, around a hundred years old? It didn't make sense. It couldn't make sense.*

I stared at the photograph, trying to force my mind to process what I was seeing. Could it be him? The resemblance was too uncanny. I took a step back, the weight of the moment pressing down on me.

Suddenly, the rocking chair beside me groaned, as if someone—or something—had just sat down.

I froze, my breath catching in my throat. The chair swayed, barely noticeable at first, but enough to send a jolt of terror through my chest. It hadn't moved before—or maybe I hadn't noticed—but now it creaked again, as if someone had just risen from it.

The air around me grew unnaturally cold, the kind of chill that seeped deep into my bones. I tightened my grip on the flashlight instinctively, my pulse quickening as the heavy silence settled in once again.

The beam flickered.

My breath hitched. Panic began to bloom in my chest, a creeping, uncontrollable feeling. My mind raced through the possibilities, but none of them made sense.

Suddenly, a sharp crack pierced the silence.

I jerked around, my body reacting before my mind could catch up. My pulse hammered in my ears, the sound of the gunshot still ringing—a gunshot. My head snapped toward the sound, toward the chair. I stared at it, my breath coming in shallow gasps.

And then I saw it.

Blood.

A dark stain smeared across the back of the chair, slowly trickling downward, almost hidden by the shadows but unmistakable. How could it be there? The room had been untouched. There had been no blood when I entered. I took another step back, but my legs felt heavy, like they were sinking into the floor.

Panic spread like wildfire, racing through my body, igniting every nerve. My mind whirled, trying to make sense of it—of the chair, the blood, the photo, the sound. Was it real? Was any of this real?

Had I lost my mind?

I bolted, my legs moving before I could think, the photograph clutched tight in my hand. I didn't stop until I was back in the living room, my breath ragged, my heart pounding like a drum in my ears.

A knock at the door made my heart skip a beat.

Billy.

He stood there, his usual calm demeanor shadowed by something unsettling. There was a flicker in his eyes—nervousness? Fear? "Izzy? You okay?" His voice, normally steady, wavered ever so slightly, making me wonder if he had felt it too—whatever was lurking just beneath the surface.

I could barely speak. My hand trembled as I held up the photograph. "Explain this," I managed to say, my voice hoarse.

Billy's smile faltered when he saw the picture. He stared at it for a long moment, his face unreadable. His mouth opened slightly, but no words came out at first.

"Billy... why do you look like this man?" I asked, my voice rising with fear. "This photo is from 1974. That would make you... a hundred years old."

Billy ran a hand through his hair, his brow furrowing. "I... I don't know," he muttered, his voice stumbling over the words. His eyes darted toward the photograph again, then back to me. "I swear, Izzy, I've never seen this picture before in my life."

"Don't lie to me!" I snapped, stepping closer. "That's *you*. Right there."

Billy glanced at the date again, his face pale. "I—maybe it's... I mean, maybe it's some old relative. I don't know," he stammered, his voice shaky, as if grasping at straws. Then, with a weak grin, he added, "Do I look a hundred years old, Izzy? I swear, I'm not."

His voice was steady, but the unease in his eyes told a different story. He looked confused, maybe even scared. And that frightened me even more.

Before I could ask more, a low rumble echoed from outside, rising like a distant chant, deep and gravelly, as if the earth itself was speaking. I turned toward the window. The marsh. It was alive. The air around me pulsed, and the sound grew louder, a rhythmic murmur—like a chant. Low and steady, it echoed through the ground, beating like a heartbeat: *Thrum... thrum... thrum...*

"Izzy, listen to me," Billy said, his voice sharp now. "Stay away from the marsh."

Something stirred inside me, an unfamiliar urge that I couldn't ignore. I took a step toward the door, my mind clouded with confusion, with fear, with something I couldn't explain. Billy grabbed my arm, his grip tight and desperate. "Please," he urged. "Don't go near it."

But I couldn't stop myself. I had to know.

I tore my arm free and ran out, the sound from the marsh growing louder, almost like chanting. The fog had rolled in thick, the air heavy and damp. As I moved forward, it felt like I was walking back into another time, something ancient and forgotten. I could feel the marsh watching me, pulling me closer, suffocating me.

In the reflection of the water, something shifted.

Not my face—hers. The woman from the photograph.

Hollowed eyes. Grinning.

Closer.

And she was watching me.

~ 12 ~

THE VANISHING

I stumbled back through the fog, my breath coming in shallow gasps. My heart still pounded from the sight of her—*that woman.* Hollow-eyed, grinning, getting closer in the reflection of the marsh's water. The eerie chant still echoed in my ears, as if the marsh had been calling me, pulling me into its twisted depths.

As I neared the house, the fog swirled around me, wrapping me in its cold, damp grip. The marsh's presence clung to me like a second skin, suffocating and inescapable. My thoughts were a tangled mess of fear and confusion. Every step I took toward the house felt heavier, as though I were fighting to keep my sanity. My mind kept flashing back to Billy—his warnings, his presence. I hadn't realized how much I was relying on him.

Billy warned me not to go near the marsh, pleaded with me to stay away. Yet now, more than ever, I needed answers. I needed him to explain what had just happened. But was I really trusting him? Or was I just desperate? There was always something off about him, something I couldn't quite put my finger on.

I quickened my pace, desperate to get inside, my pulse thudding against my temples. When I threw open the door, my stomach dropped. Billy was gone.

I stood frozen in the doorway, the house eerily quiet. No sign of him, no trace that he'd even been there. My eyes darted around the room, searching for something—anything—that could explain his sudden disappearance. But the only thing staring back at me was the photograph.

The cursed image I had found in the attic was now lying on the kitchen table, mocking me with its unanswered questions. It sat there like a taunt, daring me to confront the secrets it held.

I approached the table slowly, my fingers trembling as I picked up the photograph. The woman's hollow eyes seemed to follow me, her unsettling smile freezing my blood. The man who looked so much like Billy—how could he deny knowing anything about this? I ran my fingers over the worn edges, trying to make sense of it all. Why did this image affect me so much? It wasn't just the uncanny resemblance. There was something more. Something that felt... personal.

A sickening feeling twisted in my gut. The more I looked at it, the more I felt as if the photograph was trying to tell me something—something I wasn't ready to hear. Why had Billy disappeared like that? Where had he gone? He had warned me to stay away from the marsh, yet now he was the one who had vanished. It didn't make sense. None of it did.

I couldn't stay here. Not like this. I needed to talk to Micky.

Grabbing the photograph, I rushed out of the house, my heart pounding in my chest. As I pulled out of the driveway and onto the street, I glanced around, searching for Billy. But there was no sign of him. The fog clung to the edges of the road as I drove, the unsettling quiet amplifying my racing thoughts.

Why am I going to Micky's? I wondered. His shop, *Micky's Magical Things*, had always been a little unnerving, filled with oddities and whispers of things I wasn't sure I believed in. But lately, Micky had started to feel... safe. Was I really comfortable around him? Or was I just grasping at anything that felt like stability? I wasn't sure if I trusted him yet, but I needed answers. And Micky, for all his strangeness, had a way of knowing things. Maybe he could help. Or maybe I was just fooling myself.

When I arrived, the shop was quiet, the warm, comforting scent of incense filling the air. Micky was behind the counter, hunched over an old book, his face illuminated by the soft, flickering glow of a nearby lamp.

"Micky," I called softly, stepping into the shop. He looked up, his eyes immediately reading the anxiety on my face.

"Izzy? You look like you've seen a ghost," he said, half-joking, though there was concern in his voice.

"I'm starting to think I have," I muttered, setting the photograph down on the counter in front of him. "I need your help."

Micky raised an eyebrow as he picked up the photo, examining it with calm focus. "Where did you find this?" he asked, his voice steady, though I could tell he was intrigued.

"In the attic of my house. I don't know who these people are, but... that man." I pointed to the figure who looked so much like Billy. "It's him, Micky. Or at least someone who looks exactly like him. But the photo is dated 1974. How is that possible?"

Micky's face remained neutral, but I could see the gears turning. He glanced at me, waiting for more. I realized I hadn't mentioned Billy before. "Billy... he's someone I just met when I moved here. We started talking," I said quietly. "He was instantly drawn to me, and, if I'm honest, I felt drawn to him too. But there was something off, something I couldn't quite put my finger on from the start. This man in the photo—it's like looking at Billy. Exactly like him, only... this picture is from 1974. How is that even possible?"

Micky studied the photograph for a long moment before finally setting it down, his expression unreadable but now laced with curiosity.

"I've never seen a photograph of anyone who lived in that house before," he said slowly, his tone thoughtful. "But... I can look into it. See if I can dig up anything about the people in this photo."

"Please, I need to know," I said, my voice thick with desperation. "There's something wrong with that house, with the marsh... and now Billy's just gone. He was with me, trying to stop me from going near the marsh, and when I came back, he had disappeared without a word."

Micky's eyes narrowed slightly, his fingers tapping rhythmically on the counter. "Billy vanished? Just like that?"

I nodded. "I don't understand it. He seemed scared, but then... he was just gone. No explanation, no trace."

Micky didn't respond immediately. He leaned back in his chair, folding his arms across his chest, and I could feel him calculating something. He wasn't shocked by the strange events, but I couldn't read him. He had a way of hiding his thoughts until he was ready to share them—if he ever shared them.

"I'll look into the photo," he said finally, his voice more serious now. "But you need to be careful, Izzy. Whatever's going on, it's... not something you should take lightly. The marsh, the house—there's history there, and none of it's good."

"I know," I whispered, the weight of the situation pressing down on me. "But Billy—why would he leave like that? Do you think he's hiding something?"

Micky's eyes flickered with something I couldn't quite read. "It's hard to say. But I've been around long enough to know that people disappear for a reason. Sometimes, they don't want to be found."

His words sent a chill through me, but I tried to shake it off. I couldn't afford to lose myself in more paranoia. "I just need to know what's going on, Micky. Please, if you find anything... let me know."

"I will," Micky assured me, his voice soft but firm. "I'll dig around and see what I can uncover. In the meantime... stay away from that marsh."

I nodded, though deep down, I knew staying away was easier said than done. Something was calling me to that marsh, something I couldn't explain. But for now, I had no choice but to wait. And wonder.

Back at home, the house felt emptier than ever. I glanced at the spot where Billy had been standing earlier, the echoes of his warning still playing in my mind. *Where did you go, Billy?* Why had he disappeared the way he did? What was he so afraid of?

The photograph still haunted me, the woman's hollow eyes watching me from every corner of my mind. I knew I couldn't rest until I had answers—until I knew why this strange place was pulling me deeper into its mysteries.

As I sat down at the table, staring at the empty space in front of me, a cold draft swept through the room, rattling the windows. The eerie silence settled in, thick and suffocating, and I could feel it again—like a presence watching me, waiting. The marsh was out there, beyond the fog. And somewhere, Billy had vanished into it, leaving more questions than answers behind.

~ 13 ~

FIRE IN THE NIGHT

That night, I couldn't sleep. My mind was restless, circling around the photo of Billy, his face from decades ago, and yet somehow... him. It made no sense. And then, that nursery. The crib is old, really old, but there's no mention of a couple with a baby—just a couple. So why the nursery? My thoughts twisted in knots, making it impossible to rest.

I made myself a cup of chamomile tea, hoping it would calm me down, but my nerves were shot. Sitting at the kitchen table, I toyed with the cameo necklace I'd found. Its cold, smooth surface felt like the only real thing left. I stared at it, trying to focus, but my mind spiraled with the same haunting questions: *Where does Billy fit into all of this? Who were the people in that photo? And why had the nursery been left untouched for so long? The blood on the rocking chair—was that sound really a gunshot? And what did ole hollow-eyes have to do with it all?*

A sound interrupted my thoughts. A strange noise coming from outside, soft at first, then growing louder. I froze, the cup halfway to my lips. It wasn't a normal noise—no animal, no wind. It was chanting, low and rhythmic, like a group of people murmuring in unison. I stood slowly, setting the cup down on the table, my heart pounding.

I moved toward the window, my bare feet silent on the floor. Carefully, I peeked through the curtain. At first, all I saw was darkness, but then a flicker of light caught my eye. Torches—several of them—held by hooded figures moving in a line through the marsh behind my house. There were maybe ten or twelve, draped in dark capes with their faces hidden beneath deep hoods.

The chanting grew louder, and I watched in stunned silence as they made their way deeper into the marsh, the torches casting an eerie glow on the water.

Without thinking, I slipped on my shoes and quietly opened the back door. The air outside was thick with humidity, sticking to my skin as I crept after them. I knew I should stay inside, call someone, do something rational—but curiosity gnawed at me, pulling me forward. I had to know what they were doing.

I followed them through the tall grass, the smell of the marsh heavy in the air. My breath came in shallow gasps as I kept my distance, crouching low, hoping they wouldn't notice me. The chanting never stopped, a deep, almost hypnotic hum that sent chills up my spine.

They stopped at a clearing in the marsh, where the ground was dry, and formed a circle. I could see them better now, the firelight reflecting off their cloaks as they raised their torches high. The leader stood at the center of the circle, his back to me. I squinted, trying to get a better look at him, but his face was still hidden under the hood.

Suddenly, they began to move, stepping forward one by one, adding their torches to a growing fire in the middle of the clearing. The flames shot up, bright and wild, casting flickering shadows across the trees. The chanting reached a fever pitch, and I pressed my hand over my mouth, terrified that they might hear me.

Then, from the other side of the circle, they brought someone forward.

A woman.

She was struggling, her hands tied behind her back, a gag in her mouth. She thrashed against her captors, but they held her tight, forcing her toward the fire. My heart dropped into my stomach as I realized what was happening. They weren't just chanting—they were performing some kind of ritual.

A sacrifice.

The woman's eyes were wide with fear, and I felt frozen, unable to move or look away. They dragged her closer to the fire, her muffled screams barely audible over the chanting. I wanted to scream, to run, to do *something*—but I couldn't. My legs were glued to the ground, my body locked in place.

The leader raised his arms, and the chanting stopped. Silence fell over the marsh, broken only by the crackling of the fire. Slowly, almost ceremonially, he lowered his hood.

My breath caught in my throat. His face—painted, stark white, with a wide, red grin that stretched across his cheeks. His eyes were black, hollow pits, and there was a small black triangle painted on the tip of his nose—a clown. The leader of this twisted ritual had painted his face like a clown.

I stumbled back, my foot catching on a root, and I nearly fell, my heart hammering so hard I thought it might burst out of my chest. The woman was pushed to her knees in front of the fire, her sobs barely audible now. The leader pulled a knife from inside his cloak, its blade glinting in the firelight.

"No..." I whispered, too quietly for anyone to hear.

With one swift motion, he brought the knife down.

The woman's body slumped forward, lifeless.

I turned and ran. I didn't care about being quiet anymore. My feet pounded against the wet ground, my breath coming in ragged gasps as I raced back to the house. I stumbled through the back door, slamming it shut behind me, my hands shaking so hard I could barely lock it.

I pressed my back against the door, my chest heaving, trying to calm down, but the image of the clown's painted face burned in my mind. I had just watched them kill someone. But who? And why?

My whole body trembled as I made my way to the phone, but my hands were shaking too much to dial. I collapsed onto the kitchen floor, pulling my knees to my chest, my breath coming in short, panicked bursts.

Was it real? Did I really just see that? Or was I losing my mind?

I glanced at the window, half-expecting to see the hooded figures outside, but there was nothing. The marsh was still, quiet, as if nothing had happened.

But I knew what I saw. The fire, the chanting, the painted face of the clown—it was all real. And they were still out there, somewhere, in the dark.

Waiting.

I pulled my legs closer, burying my head against my knees, too terrified to move. My mind spiraled, replaying the horrifying scene—the woman's desperate eyes, the gleaming knife, the crackling fire. I stayed there all night, paralyzed, trapped in the nightmare that refused to let go.

When the sun finally rose, I was still sitting there, numb and exhausted, but alive. I didn't know what I would do next, but one thing was certain—I was in danger. And no one in this town would believe me —maybe not even Micky.

~ 14 ~

MICKY'S REVELATION

That morning, I couldn't get to Micky's shop fast enough. My heart hadn't slowed since last night; every corner of my mind was haunted by the hooded figures, the chanting, and the fear in the woman's eyes as they dragged her toward the fire, her mouth covered, unable to cry for help. I threw on the first clothes I could find and headed straight to *Micky's Magical Things*, my hands still trembling as I pushed open the door.

The familiar scent of burning sage and the clutter of ancient relics greeted me, but even the comforting atmosphere of Micky's shop wasn't enough to calm the terror gnawing at me. Micky stood behind the counter, looking up with his usual gentle smile, but his expression shifted to concern as soon as he saw my face.

"Izzy, my dear, you look as if you've seen the devil himself," he said, his rich English accent doing little to soothe the tension running through me.

I forced a shaky smile. "I might have," I replied, my voice barely above a whisper.

Micky frowned and gestured to the chair by the counter. "Come, sit. Tell me everything."

I sat down, my legs still feeling like they could give out at any moment. The words poured out of me—every terrifying detail from the night before: the hooded figures, the torches, the fire, the woman's death, and the leader's painted face. As I spoke, Micky's expression grew darker, more serious than I had ever seen him.

When I finished, the room felt suffocatingly silent. Micky leaned back in his chair, rubbing his chin thoughtfully. His usual light-hearted demeanor had vanished, replaced by something more somber.

"Izzy," he began slowly, "what you've described isn't just some nightmare. It sounds like something far older and darker than anyone would believe."

"What do you mean?" I asked, leaning forward, my pulse quickening.

Micky stood and walked over to one of the cluttered shelves, his fingers trailing over the dusty spines of old books. He pulled down one of the thick, ancient volumes and set it carefully on the counter. It looked fragile, like it might crumble if handled too roughly. He flipped through its pages, pausing at a section that seemed to catch his eye.

"This book," he said, "is one of the oldest I have, detailing the darker history of Bayou Vista—before it became the town we know today." He paused, tapping the page with a long finger. "The land your house sits on, Izzy, wasn't always just quiet marshland. Long ago, it was used for... well, devil worship."

My stomach dropped, and I felt a cold shiver run down my spine. "Devil worship?" I whispered.

He nodded grimly. "Centuries ago, secret cults would gather on that land, performing dark rituals—sacrifices to summon evil forces. The land itself became tainted, cursed, if you believe the stories. The last of these rituals was said to have ended long before the town was officially founded, but it seems like something has awakened it again."

I shuddered at the thought, my mind flashing back to the horrifying scene of the hooded figures and the woman's death. "The leader's face," I whispered, "it was painted like a clown. Does that mean anything?"

Micky's eyes narrowed. "Clowns were often used in old ritualistic ceremonies to mock purity, to distort innocence into something grotesque. In many cultures, they represent chaos, a kind of malevolent trickery. Whoever this leader is, they're not just performing a ritual—they're taunting something deeper, something dark."

I could barely process his words, but one thing stuck in my mind. "Micky, in the house... there's an old nursery—a crib that looks ancient, like it's been untouched for years. No one ever mentioned a couple with a baby—just the couple living there. Could there be any history of a baby connected to that land?"

Micky frowned, considering my question. "A baby?" He shook his head. "Not that I've come across. But I'll dig deeper. There's still more to learn, especially about that photo you found. I've been looking into it, but no concrete answers just yet."

A wave of disappointment washed over me, but I knew if anyone could uncover the truth, it would be Micky. He had a way of finding answers when others gave up. Still, the thought of a baby, of that untouched nursery, gnawed at me. There had to be something there, some clue I was missing.

Micky looked at me again, his eyes soft with concern. "Izzy, you don't have to face this alone. If you want, I can come with you and help you sort through everything. But really, you don't have to go back at all. I have an extra bedroom upstairs, and you're more than welcome to stay here until we understand what's going on."

His offer was kind, a tempting escape from the nightmare that had gripped my life. For a moment, I considered it—staying in Micky's extra bedroom, far away from the house and the horrors it held. But could I really just leave it behind? I hesitated, the thought of returning to that house—the marsh, the fire, the hooded figures—still fresh in my mind, making my stomach churn. Part of me wanted Micky to come with me, to have someone else witness what I had seen, something too terrifying to face alone. But another part of me wasn't sure if what I'd witnessed was even real. Maybe the isolation, the strange events, and the dark history of the place were warping my mind, twisting reality into something it wasn't.

"I don't know..." I muttered, unable to meet his eyes.

Micky tilted his head, waiting patiently. "It's your decision, Izzy. But if you feel unsafe, I'll be there in a heartbeat."

I nodded, though I still couldn't answer. *Did I really want to go back? And if I did, what would I find waiting for me?*

The silence between us stretched, broken only by the soft ticking of an old clock on the wall. Micky stood quietly, watching me, giving me the space to process everything.

Finally, I looked up, my voice steady despite the fear gnawing at me. "Micky, the land—the history you mentioned. Is there any connection to the LaBlanc family? I found a journal belonging to Mary LaBlanc. She wrote that the house had been passed down for generations and even referred to herself as 'the queen.'"

Micky's eyes darkened at the mention of her name, and he flipped through the book again, his fingers lingering over certain passages. "The LaBlancs were well-known in Bayou Vista," he said slowly. "Prominent family, lots of money, but also a lot of secrets. Mary LaBlanc, in particular, was a bit of a local legend—some even called her eccentric. From what I've gathered, they weren't directly involved in the old rituals, but there were whispers that some branches of the family dabbled in... darker practices. Nothing proven, though."

I leaned forward. "So, they might've known about the land's history?"

"Possibly," Micky said, closing the book with a heavy thud. "But that journal of hers might hold more clues than we realize. They were connected to a lot of strange happenings over the years, but no one ever confirmed anything. It's likely they knew more than they let on."

I swallowed hard, my mind racing. The LaBlancs, the dark history of the land, the hooded figures—it all felt connected, like pieces of a puzzle I couldn't quite fit together.

Micky's voice broke through my thoughts. "If there's a connection to the LaBlanc family, I'll find it. But be careful, Izzy. Whatever's happening out there—it's not done yet."

His words sent a chill through me, and I stood, my legs unsteady. "Thanks, Micky. I'll... I'll think about your offer."

He nodded, watching me closely. "Take care of yourself, Izzy. And if you need anything—anything at all—you know where to find me."

I left the shop feeling no more at ease than when I had entered. If anything, Micky's revelation had only deepened my sense of dread. Devil worship, dark rituals, and a cursed land—all connected to the place I now call home.

As I walked back through the quiet streets of Bayou Vista, my thoughts kept returning to the nursery. The crib, so old and untouched, as if waiting for a child that never came. And then the photo—Billy, or someone who looked exactly like him, standing there in a moment frozen in time. But how could it be him?

I shuddered, the morning sunlight doing little to warm the cold fear that had settled deep inside me. Whatever was happening on that land, it wasn't finished with me yet. And I wasn't sure if I was ready to face it.

By the time I reached my front door, I still hadn't made a decision. Could I really face the horrors of last night again, with Micky by my side? Or would I be risking dragging him into something far worse?

The house stood silent, looming before me, as if it were waiting for my next move.

I took a deep breath, steeling myself for whatever was coming next.

Because I knew, deep down, it wasn't over. Not by a long shot.

~ 15 ~

STRANGE HAPPENINGS

That night, the house felt different. It had always been unsettling, ever since I'd moved in, but tonight... tonight it was alive. I tried to convince myself that it was just the stress. Micky's warning played on repeat in my mind, but I couldn't shake the feeling that the house had been waiting for something.

It was waiting for me.

The wind howled outside, rattling the old windows, but inside the house, there was another kind of noise. I sat on the edge of my bed, staring at the walls, listening. It was subtle at first, barely noticeable—a soft, distant sound. I strained to hear it over the storm outside. And then it became clear.

A baby.

Crying.

My breath caught in my throat. I froze, every hair on my body standing on end. There was no baby in this house. There hadn't been a baby here for generations, as far as I knew. Yet, the sound was unmistakable—a soft, desperate wail drifting from upstairs—the nursery.

I didn't move at first. I sat there, my hands clenched into fists on my knees, trying to convince myself that I was imagining it. Maybe it was the wind, or an animal outside. But the cry grew louder, more insistent, tugging at my nerves like fingers pulling me out of bed.

Against every ounce of logic, I stood up. My feet moved on their own, carrying me out of my room and into the hallway. The walls seemed to close in around me as I walked, the shadows stretching longer, darker. The house creaked with every step, as if it were breathing.

I reached the stairs. The crying continued, now a pitiful, echoing sob that bounced off the walls. My legs trembled as I started to climb, each step feeling heavier than the last. The air grew colder the higher I went, until it felt like I was walking into an icebox. The closer I got to the nursery, the louder the sound became—heartbreaking, eerie, unnatural.

I reached the door, my hand hovering over the knob. The crying stopped. Silence.

I stood there for a moment, my hand trembling, wondering if I had finally lost my mind. Then, from somewhere deep in the house, came a sudden, sharp *BANG*.

A gunshot.

I gasped, my hand flying to my mouth. It came from the attic.

My pulse thundered in my ears as I turned toward the attic door at the end of the hallway. The sound had been too real, too clear to ignore. My feet dragged me down the hall, my eyes locked on the door. Something deep inside was pulling at me, begging me not to open the door again. I had just been up there, but whatever was in that attic... it was calling me back, demanding that I face it.

I reached the attic door, my hand trembling as I grasped the cold knob. Slowly, I turned it, the creak of the door louder than I expected, slicing through the silence. The stairs leading up were steep, and the darkness at the top was thick and heavy. I couldn't see anything beyond the first few steps.

I climbed slowly, my heart pounding so hard I thought it might burst from my chest. As I reached the top, I saw her.

The young woman from the picture.

She was sitting in the old rocking chair, her head slumped to the side. Her pale face, framed by dark curls, was streaked with dried blood. A single bullet wound marred her temple, and on the floor beside her, there was a gun, the barrel pointed toward her feet. She looked peaceful, almost as if she were sleeping, but the stillness of her body said otherwise.

My knees nearly buckled beneath me. I felt my stomach twist, my breath coming in short, ragged gasps as I tried to process what I was seeing. This wasn't possible. It couldn't be.

But it was.

I backed away slowly, unable to tear my eyes from the lifeless figure in the chair. I stumbled down the stairs, my hand gripping the railing to keep from collapsing.

Just as I reached the bottom, I froze.

She was there.

The woman with the hollow eyes—the one I had seen before, in the mirror, in the reflection of the water, in the photograph at the bottom of the stairs. It was Mary LaBlanc. She stood at the doorway of one of the bedrooms, her skeletal face contorted in a horrifying mix of sorrow and anger. Her hollow, empty eyes locked onto mine, cold and unrelenting. I was frozen. I couldn't move. I couldn't breathe.

We stared at each other for what felt like an eternity. Her mouth moved, but no sound came out. It was like she was trying to speak, to tell me something, but the words were trapped in her throat.

Then, in a blink, she was gone.

I gasped, stumbling back into the hallway, my heart racing. My hands shook violently as I pressed myself against the wall, trying to steady my breath. I closed my eyes, willing it all to stop, hoping I was just hallucinating, that it was all some terrible dream.

But then I heard it again.

The whispers.

They came from the walls, from the floors, from every corner of the house. Faint, hushed voices, rising and falling like chanting, speaking words I couldn't understand. The air around me thickened, pressing down on my chest like an invisible hand. I darted down the stairs, back to my room, slamming the door behind me.

I stood there, my back against the door, panting, my body trembling uncontrollably. I glanced around the room, hoping to find some sense of normalcy, but objects began to shift on their own. The lamp on the nightstand flickered and then fell to the floor with a loud crash. The curtains moved as if caught in a breeze, though the windows were shut tight. My closet door creaked open slowly, revealing only darkness within.

I was losing my mind. I had to be.

The whispers got louder, overlapping into a mess of sounds—voices and words—too many at once. I clutched my head, trying to block them out, but they only grew more insistent, more violent. My vision blurred, and my breath came in shallow gasps. The room spun around me, the walls closing in.

I felt eyes on me. Watching. Always watching.

I sank to the floor, my hands shaking uncontrollably. My mind was unraveling, slipping away piece by piece. I could feel it. I was no longer alone in this house. The spirits—whatever they were—they were here, and they wanted something from me.

I closed my eyes tightly, curling into myself, trying to block out the sounds, the movements, the eyes. But they were everywhere. The house was alive with them.

For what felt like hours, I stayed there on the floor, trapped in a waking nightmare. I tried to tell myself it wasn't real, that it was all in my head. But deep down, I knew the truth.

When I finally opened my eyes, the whispers had stopped. The room was still, the objects unmoved. But I could feel it—the presence, the darkness, lingering in the air like a thick fog.

I didn't know how much longer I could take it. My mind was fraying at the edges, and I wasn't sure if I could survive another night here.

I stood up slowly, my legs weak beneath me. I needed to get out. I needed to leave, to get as far away from this house as possible. But something kept me there, rooted to the spot. The house wouldn't let me go. It held me in its grasp, tightening its grip with each passing moment.

This house wasn't just haunted. It was cursed.

And it wanted me.

~ 16 ~

ISOLATION

The next few days blurred together, each one heavier than the last. I drifted through them, feeling like I was slipping further from reality. My body ached, my head was clouded, and I couldn't focus. The house felt oppressive, the air thick and stifling, as if it was closing in on me. I hadn't seen Billy in what felt like forever, and I wasn't sure if he had really vanished or if my mind was playing tricks on me. Nothing felt real anymore.

When he finally reappeared, something about him had changed—something darker, something that sent a chill up my spine. It wasn't anything obvious. He still smiled, still spoke the same way he always had, but there was an unsettling undercurrent. His charm had soured, and his presence now felt suffocating.

One evening, after yet another long stretch of silence between us, I couldn't hold back any longer. "Where were you?" I asked, my voice tight with frustration. "You just... disappeared. No word, nothing."

Billy leaned back in his chair, his smile not quite reaching his eyes. His body language was too relaxed for how tense I felt. There was a subtle shift in his posture, his movements deliberate, as if he was controlling the space between us. "Disappeared? Izzy, I've been right here. You're so wrapped up in this house, I guess you didn't even notice me coming and going. What's really going on with you?"

I blinked, trying to make sense of his words. "No, I did notice. It's like you weren't here. You just... vanished."

Billy's smile widened, but it didn't comfort me. It felt wrong, like there was something underneath it I couldn't pinpoint. He stood up, stepping closer, his voice dropping to a soft, almost mocking tone. His eyes narrowed slightly as he studied me. "Or maybe you imagined it. You've been hearing things, right? Maybe it's all in your head."

His words hit me like a slap. I opened my mouth to argue, but doubt flooded my mind. Was it all in my head? I had been hearing things—the whispers, the strange noises—but they were real, weren't they?

"I—" I stammered, feeling unsteady. "But you were gone. You can't just—"

Billy's expression shifted, his eyes sharper now, like he was watching me carefully. "Are you sure, Izzy? Or is this just like the voices? The things you've been hearing that no one else can? You've been... off lately. I think you're seeing things."

Was he right? Could I really be imagining everything? My body screamed no, but my mind whispered otherwise. The noises, the strange happenings—they had felt real. But if Billy was telling the truth... if I really was losing my grip, then what could I trust?

I shook my head, trying to focus. His presence was overwhelming, pressing in on me. "No, that's not it. I know what I saw."

"You worry too much." His voice was low, almost soothing, but there was a dangerous edge to it. "The town's been filling your head with nonsense. They don't want you to know the truth."

A knot of unease twisted in my stomach. "What truth?"

His smile vanished, replaced by something colder, more menacing. "They're hiding things from you. They've been keeping secrets for years. They want to control you, keep you blind to what's really going on."

I frowned, dread creeping into my thoughts. "That's not true. Micky—"

"Micky?" Billy's voice turned sharp, his sneer unmistakable. He took another step closer, and the air between us felt charged with tension. "You can't trust him. He's part of it. Part of their lies."

His words sent a wave of nausea through me. Micky had been the only one in town who'd shown me real kindness, who'd tried to help. But Billy's certainty gnawed at my thoughts. Could he be right? Was there more to the town than I realized?

Still, something felt off. The way Billy spoke, the way he watched me—it didn't sit right. "Billy, I think you're wrong. You're not making sense."

He stepped closer again, his voice dropping to a near-whisper, but the threat was clear. "They're turning you against me, Izzy. They want to make you doubt me. Don't let them. You belong here... with me."

The room seemed to shrink, his words hanging in the air like a weight I couldn't shake. I wanted to believe he was looking out for me, that I could trust him, but something about the way he was talking, the way his eyes gleamed—it felt dangerous. His charm had become something darker, something that made my skin crawl.

"I need some air," I muttered, stepping back toward the door, my heart racing. I couldn't breathe. I needed to get out, away from him, away from the suffocating tension that had settled between us.

Billy didn't stop me. He just watched as I slipped out the door, his dark smile lingering in my mind long after I'd left.

The air outside was thick with humidity, but it felt better than the atmosphere inside the house. I leaned against the porch railing, trying to calm my racing heart. Even with the night air around me, there was a chill that seemed to cling to my skin, an eerie reminder of the house behind me. The whispers crept back, swirling in the corners of my mind, louder than before.

Don't trust him, they seemed to say. Don't trust anyone.

After that night, I withdrew from everyone—Billy, the town, even Micky. The house became my refuge, though it felt far from safe. The strange occurrences inside its walls only grew worse, but I couldn't bear to leave. I avoided the townsfolk, their whispers, their curious stares. I stayed hidden, but the house knew. It thrived on my isolation.

Every night at 3:33 a.m., the house and the Marsh would come alive—the air thick with the unsettling hum of chanting from the ritual outside. I learned not to look, to keep the curtains drawn tight, and never, under any circumstances, open the door when the knocking started. The sounds grew louder with each passing night. Each creak in the floorboards, every faint whisper of movement, felt like something was drawing closer, as if the house itself was tightening its grip on me. The coldness of the place seeped into my bones, chilling me to the core. Sometimes, I swore I heard footsteps above me, pacing in the attic. But every time I went to check, there was nothing. Just emptiness, the silence mocking me, leaving me wondering how much longer I could take it.

The voices never stopped. They lingered, soft breaths against my skin, too faint to grasp but impossible to ignore. Sometimes I thought I heard my name, but it was always too distant to be sure. I tried to convince myself it wasn't real, but the line between reality and my mind had begun to blur.

My body was breaking down. Sleep was impossible with the constant whispers, and food made me sick. Pain radiated through my back, my muscles weak and sore, like a sickness slowly taking hold. I avoided mirrors. I knew I wouldn't recognize myself, the hollow version of who I'd become.

One night, the house felt more alive than ever. I was sitting in the living room, staring at the flickering lamp in the corner. The air was thick, heavy with tension, but it wasn't the warmth that pressed down on me—it was the cold. It wasn't the voices that scared me anymore; it was the silence between them, the waiting. The chill seemed to crawl through the walls, slipping beneath my skin. The lamp flickered, its light barely reaching the edges of the room. The darkness wasn't just there—it was alive, closing in around me.

Then I heard it—a soft creak from the hallway. My heart stuttered in my chest, the cold intensifying. Another creak. Closer.

"Billy?" I whispered, but my voice felt swallowed by the weight of the air. I stood, legs trembling as I moved toward the hallway. Nothing. Just emptiness.

The creaking continued, steady, like someone was walking toward me. My pulse quickened, my breath shallow. The whispers returned, louder now, filling the air with their insistent murmurs.

Then—a breath. Right behind me.

My chest tightened, my vision blurred, and for a moment, I thought I saw something moving, crawling toward me.

I pulled out my phone, my finger hovering over my friend's name—Donna. She'd been trying to reach me for days. But what could I tell her? That I was hearing voices? That the house was watching me? She wouldn't understand. No one would. With a deep breath, I scrolled down until Micky's name appeared on the screen. I stared at it, the glow from his number filling the room. What if Billy was right? What if I couldn't trust Micky either? My heart pounded in my chest, doubt creeping in, suffocating me.

That was the last time I tried reaching out.

The days blended into nights, time losing all meaning as I stared out at the marsh from my window. Bayou Vista felt distant, like a dream I couldn't quite remember. Even my memories of life before the house seemed out of reach.

Billy came back, but he was even more changed. His charm had faded, replaced by something cold and possessive. Every glance felt like he was waiting for me to break.

I was alone, trapped in the house. Isolated from everyone. And the house knew it.

I wasn't sure how much longer I could hold on. The darkness inside me had grown, and it was swallowing everything in its path. There had to be a way out... but I couldn't see it anymore.

~ 17 ~

THE DOCTOR'S VISIT

It's been four weeks since Billy disappeared—again. Four long, grueling weeks, and every day since has been worse than the last. I've barely slept. Every night, I lie there, wide awake, staring at the ceiling while my mind spins and my body aches. I can't remember the last time I ate anything that didn't make me feel sick. And the pain... It's like something is gnawing at me from the inside—my back, my kidneys, my muscles, everything hurts.

But the worst part is my head. It's like a fog has settled in, thick and impenetrable. I can't focus on anything. Simple tasks take hours because I keep losing track of what I'm doing. I'll start washing dishes and then find myself standing in the hallway with no idea how I got there. It's like my mind isn't mine anymore. And then there are the voices. Quiet at first, like a low murmur in the distance, but lately, they've been louder. Closer. Sometimes I can almost make out what they're saying. But every time I try to listen, they slip away.

I finally broke down and made an appointment with Dr. Wilson in the nearby town of Cypress Cove. I don't know what I expected, but maybe I thought he'd have some answers, something to explain why I feel like this. Something more than what's in my head.

The waiting room at his office is cold and sterile, like the air has been sucked out, leaving nothing but the hum of the fluorescent lights. My hands tremble in my lap, my chest tight, each breath shallow as if I can't get enough air. The pounding in my head is relentless, like someone's beating a drum behind my eyes. I try to push it away, focus on calming myself, but I can't stop my leg from bouncing nervously as I wait for my name to be called.

The receptionist, a young woman with glasses too big for her face, finally calls my name. I stand, my legs wobbling under me. It feels like I might collapse with every step as I follow her down the long hallway.

Dr. Wilson is already sitting behind his desk when I enter. He's an older man, with graying hair and deep lines etched into his face. He smiles when I walk in, "Izzy, come in," he says, gesturing to the chair across from him. "How are you today?"

I sink into the chair, my body heavy, like I'm carrying the weight of the world. My hands feel clammy as I wipe them on my jeans, trying to stop the shaking. "I don't know," I say, my voice shaky. "I feel... awful. I can't sleep, I can't eat, my body hurts all over. My back, my kidneys, it's like everything is just... shutting down."

He leans forward, his brow furrowing as he jots something down on his notepad. "Have you been under any unusual stress lately?"

I almost laugh, but it comes out as more of a scoff. Stress doesn't begin to cover it. "I guess you could say that."

"Tell me about it," he says, setting the notepad aside and folding his hands on the desk. "Sometimes the body reacts to stress in ways that can mimic illness."

I hesitate, trying to figure out where to start. *Should I mention Billy? The way he just disappeared without a word? Or the voices I've been hearing? Or the nightmares?* I settle on something simple. "I moved recently. To Devil's Marsh."

His eyes widen slightly, just for a second, before he masks it with a professional nod. "That's quite the place," he says, his voice neutral. "I've heard some stories about it."

"Yeah, well... it hasn't exactly been easy adjusting. The house feels... wrong, somehow. I don't know how to explain it. Like there's something off. And ever since I moved in, I've been feeling worse. Weak, achy, like I'm coming down with something, but it never gets better."

He nods slowly. "We'll run some tests to be sure, but everything you're describing could be linked to stress and anxiety. It can take a serious toll on the body."

I clench my hands together in my lap, trying to steady the trembling. The dull throb behind my eyes intensifies, and for a second, I wonder if I'm about to faint. *He's too calm, too sure that I'm fine. But what if he's hiding something?*

What if he knows there's something wrong with me but doesn't want to tell me?

"But what about the pain? My kidneys? My back? It feels real," I blurt out, the words sounding more desperate than I intended.

Dr. Wilson taps his pen on the desk, considering my words. "Pain can be psychosomatic, Izzy. The brain is powerful. If you're under a lot of stress, it can manifest physically. The tests will help rule out anything serious, but from what you're telling me, it could be your body reacting to whatever is going on in your mind."

I feel a knot tighten in my chest. *Psychosomatic. That word feels wrong. Like it's all in my head. But this pain is real. The weakness, the exhaustion—it's real.*

"And the voices?" I say, my voice barely above a whisper. "I've been hearing things. Whispers. Sometimes it sounds like someone's calling my name, but when I turn around, there's no one there."

Dr. Wilson doesn't look surprised, which somehow makes it worse. "Auditory hallucinations can also be a symptom of extreme stress. Especially if you're not sleeping well. Sleep deprivation can cause all sorts of disturbances."

I shake my head, my heart pounding. My hands are still shaking, and I feel the pounding in my head intensifying. *Is he right? Am I really imagining all of this? Or is there something darker at play that no test will ever find?* "But what if it's not just stress? What if there's something wrong with me? Something you're not seeing?"

He sighs, leaning back in his chair. "Izzy, I understand how frightening this must be. We'll run every test we can, but I want you to know that a lot of what you're describing can be linked to anxiety. It's not uncommon for people who are going through difficult times to experience symptoms like this."

I stare at him, my mind racing. *Anxiety? Stress? Is that really what's happening to me? Or is there something darker at play? Something lurking beneath the surface that no test can find?*

I leave the office with a prescription for anti-anxiety medication and a gnawing feeling in my gut that none of this will help. As I walk to my car, I can still hear the doctor's voice in my head, telling me I'm fine. But I don't feel fine. I feel like I'm unraveling.

On the way home, I stop at Berry's Market, hoping the fresh air and the mundane act of grocery shopping will clear my head. But the second I step inside, the fluorescent lights feel too bright, the aisles too narrow. My head is pounding again, and my hands are shaking as I grip the basket. My breath catches in my chest, shallow and fast, like I can't get enough air. The faint murmurs of the other shoppers blur together into an incoherent buzz. I grab a basket and start walking down the aisles, not even looking at the shelves. My hands move automatically, picking up cans of soup, crackers, whatever I can reach. But the whole time, I'm muttering to myself, replaying the doctor's words over and over.

"Everything looks normal, Izzy."

Normal? How can everything be normal when I feel like this?

"Need any help, hon?"

I blink, realizing I've stopped in front of the bakery. Stefanie Jordan, or Firecracker as most people call her, is standing behind the counter, giving me a concerned look. Her hair is covered with a baseball cap, and there's flour dusting her apron.

I force a smile, but it feels weak. "No, I'm fine."

She raises an eyebrow, clearly not convinced. "You sure?"

I almost laugh at that. If only she knew. But instead, I just nod and move on, feeling her eyes on my back. I know she's suspicious. I can feel it in the way she watches me as I walk away.

Up front, the cashiers, Taylor McCray and Laurrie McBride, are whispering to each other, their eyes darting in my direction. Firecracker must have said something to them because now they're watching me, too. Everyone's watching. It feels like the whole town is keeping tabs on me, like they know something I don't.

I go through Taylor's line, and she tries to make small talk, asking how I'm doing. I mutter something back, not even sure what I'm saying. My mind is elsewhere, re-playing the doctor's visit, over and over. *"You're fine, Izzy. You're fine."* But I'm not fine. I'm not even close.

On the drive back home, my hands are trembling on the steering wheel, my breath coming in shallow gasps. I pass Micky's shop. He's outside, locking the door, and for a split second, I think about pulling over. About asking him what the hell is really going on. But Billy's voice echoes in my head again: *"Don't trust him. Don't trust anyone."* Why would Billy say that? Why warn me against Micky?

I keep driving.

When I get home, the house is as cold and silent as ever. The shadows in the corners seem darker, the air heavier. My phone lights up with a call from Donna, but I let it go to voicemail. I can't talk to her. I can't talk to anyone.

I sit at the kitchen table, staring at the wall, feeling the weight of the world pressing down on me. My eyes drift to the window, and for a moment, I think I see a figure outside. A shadow moving through the marsh. But when I blink, it's gone.

The doctor's words creep back into my mind, taunting me. *"You're fine."*

But I'm not fine. And I don't think I ever will be again.

~ 18 ~

THE ATTIC

It was late, and the kitchen was quiet except for the soft hum of the fridge. I sat there, staring into my tea. My nerves were still on edge, despite the heavy dose of anti-anxiety medication the doctor had prescribed. The air in the house felt thick tonight—heavier than usual, like it was pressing down on my chest, making it hard to breathe. There was a faint musty smell too, like damp wood and old fabric. It had been lingering for days, but I kept telling myself it was just an old house settling into its bones.

Then I heard it—faint, but unmistakable. A soft, muffled sound like someone crying. I froze, straining to listen. It came again, clearer this time. A woman's sobs, echoing faintly through the walls.

At first, I thought it was the wind rattling the windows or maybe just the creaks and groans of this ancient place. But no, it was real. My heart began to race, and every instinct told me to stay put, to stay where it was safe, but something about the cry tugged at me. Slowly, I got up, the chair scraping against the floor, the sound almost deafening in the quiet of the house.

The crying was coming from upstairs.

Each step I took made the old wood floor creak beneath me, the sounds echoing like whispers in the dark. The further I went, the colder the air grew, like the house was sinking into some kind of deep, frozen abyss. My skin prickled as if someone was watching me. But I was alone—or at least, I should have been.

The sound of the crying led me down the long, dark hallway. That hallway had always felt wrong, unnaturally cold. And tonight, it felt even worse. The shadows seemed to stretch out, flickering like something was moving just out of my line of sight. My breath caught in my throat as I approached the attic door.

I hesitated, my fingers hovering over the doorknob. There had been something off about the attic since the day I moved in. I'd heard noises before—scratching, the occasional thud—but I brushed it off, trying to convince myself it was just the wind or animals. But this? This was different. This was real.

Slowly, I twisted the knob, my hand cold and clammy, and pushed the door open. The air in the attic was even colder than the rest of the house, a chill that sank deep into my bones. It smelled of dust and rot, the kind of smell that makes your stomach turn. Something else hung in the air too—something sour, like decay.

I climbed the small set of stairs, each step groaning under my weight. There, in the middle of the dimly lit room, sat the blood-stained rocking chair. And in that chair was a young woman, her body curled in on itself, her long, dark hair matted and hanging in her face. She was sobbing, her shoulders trembling with every broken breath. She couldn't have been more than eighteen, maybe nineteen, and a chilling sense of familiarity washed over me. My eyes widened in horror—it looked like the young girl from the picture. The same hollow eyes, the same dark hair. My blood turned to ice as I realized I was staring at the girl whose face had haunted me for days. I froze, my blood turning to ice.

She looked up at me then, her eyes wide and tear-streaked. There was something desperate in those eyes, something broken. "Can you help me?" she whispered, her voice trembling, barely more than a breath.

I couldn't move. My throat had gone dry, and my heart hammered in my chest. "W-What do you need?" I managed to stammer, though my legs felt like they would give out at any second.

"My mom... she's so angry," the girl said, her voice breaking. She seemed to be choking on the words, like they were too painful to say out loud. "I told her about the boy from town—the one who got me pregnant. He comes from a rich family, and at first, she was happy. She told me everything would be okay, that she'd help me raise the baby. But when I gave birth..."

She paused, and I could see the terror in her eyes. She was shaking all over now. "...the baby didn't look anything like him." Her voice cracked again, and fresh tears streamed down her face.

"My mom confronted him," she continued. "He swore he never even touched me. Said he barely knew who I was. And then... she called my baby a bastard. She told me she was going to get rid of it. She said the father was probably some lowlife from Pelican's Bay."

A shiver ran down my spine, the kind that made me want to turn and run. But I couldn't move. My feet were glued to the floor. "What happened to the baby?" I asked, my voice shaking.

The girl's lips trembled. "She took him. I never saw him again." Her voice cracked, and she began to sob uncontrollably. "But my mom... she's going to find out who the father is, and when she does..."

My stomach tightened. "Who is the father?" I asked, even though I wasn't sure I wanted to know.

The girl shook her head violently, her sobs turning hysterical. "I can't... I can't tell her. I can't face her. I can't... do this."

Before I could react, she pulled out a gun. My breath caught in my throat, and my body went cold. "Wait—don't do this! Please, don't!" I begged, my hands trembling as I stepped closer. But my feet felt like lead, my voice so weak I knew she couldn't hear the desperation in it.

Her eyes met mine—hollow, broken, and filled with a kind of sorrow I couldn't even begin to understand. "I'm sorry," she whispered, and then, before I could stop her, she pulled the trigger.

The gunshot exploded through the attic, a deafening crack that echoed in my ears. Blood sprayed the wall behind her, splattering onto the dusty floor. Her body slumped forward in the chair, her hand limp, the gun falling to the floor with a dull thud.

I stood there, frozen, the world spinning around me. I couldn't scream. I couldn't move. My legs felt weak, like they would give out at any moment. The smell of blood filled the air, mixing with the stench of decay, choking me.

I stumbled back, crashing into a stack of old boxes, gasping for air. I had to get out. I had to leave. But before I could move, I heard it—a soft creak, like footsteps on the stairs. Slow, deliberate, coming toward the attic.

No. No, no, no...

I turned, and there he was—the clown. The same grotesque figure from the marsh, the same face I saw before everything went black that night. His white face twisted into a grotesque grin, his eyes cold and lifeless. The air seemed to freeze around him, the temperature dropping even further. I could feel the sweat on my skin turning cold as ice.

He didn't say a word. He just stared at me for what felt like an eternity, and then he turned, walking down the hallway, toward the bedrooms.

I couldn't stop myself. I followed, my body moving on its own, my mind screaming at me to run, to get out of this house, but my feet wouldn't listen. I watched him step into the first bedroom. There, in the bed, a young man lay sleeping, unaware of the terror looming over him.

The clown raised his machete, his movements slow and methodical. I wanted to scream, to do anything to stop him, but my throat was locked tight with fear. The blade came down, slicing clean through the man's throat. Blood sprayed across the room, painting the walls in a sickening crimson. The man didn't even have time to scream.

I stumbled back, bile rising in my throat. *Oh God. Oh God.*

But it wasn't over. The clown moved to the next room, where another man slept. I watched in horror as he repeated the same brutal act, the blade cutting through flesh and bone with a sickening ease. Blood soaked the sheets, the smell of death filling the air.

And then, there was the old woman's room, the one with the hollowed eyes. She was already awake, her eyes wide with terror as he entered. She opened her mouth to scream, but he moved faster, grabbing a pillow and pressing it over her face, smothering her until her body went limp.

I couldn't breathe. My chest felt like it was going to explode. My mind was spinning, and I could barely think.

I had to get out. I had to leave this place before he saw me.

But then... he turned. His cold, dead eyes locked on me.

Run.

I bolted down the stairs, my legs barely carrying me as I stumbled toward the door. My breath came in ragged gasps, my heart pounding so hard I thought it might burst out of my chest. I grabbed my keys off the counter, tearing the door open, the cool night air slapping me in the face.

My hands shook as I fumbled with the car keys. I glanced back at the house, half expecting to see him standing there. But the porch was empty. The house stood still and silent, as if it hadn't just witnessed the horror inside.

I didn't wait to find out if he was coming. I slammed the car door shut, my hands trembling as I turned the ignition. The tires squealed as I pulled out of the driveway, my heart still pounding, my skin slick with cold sweat.

But even as the house disappeared behind me, the terror clung to me. Wrapping itself around my throat, choking me.

Something was wrong with that place. Something far worse than I could ever have imagined.

$$\sim 19 \sim$$

MICKY'S WARNING

I pulled into the parking lot of Micky's Magical Things at 4:30 in the morning, the dashboard clock casting an eerie green glow over the darkness outside. It must have been 3:33 when all this occurred—that unsettling moment when the house came alive, as it always did. But why that time? The thought gnawed at me, the strange significance of it twisting my mind.

The shop stood silent, its shutters down, and a crooked *Closed* sign hung in the window. Everything felt off, like the world had shifted, and I was the only one caught between it all. I had nowhere else to go.

Sitting in my car, I kept my eyes on the darkened shop, my thoughts racing back to the horrors in Devil's Marsh: Billy, the murders, the clown's dead eyes, and the blood. All of it churned in my mind, refusing to settle. My heart was pounding, and my hands trembled as I gripped the steering wheel.

Micky had to know something—*anything*—that could make sense of this nightmare.

The hours crawled by as I fought against the sleep that never came. My mind drifted, but every time I closed my eyes, I was back in that attic with the girl. Her pale face, her hollow eyes just before the gun went off. And then the clown's painted face staring right through me.

Finally, as the first sliver of dawn pierced the horizon, I saw movement. The shop's door creaked open, and there he was—Micky, wearing his worn leather jacket, his hair wild, eyes sharp even at this early hour. He seemed to sense my presence before he even saw me, tilting his head in that knowing way of his.

I stepped out of the car, my legs heavy, my mind swirling. Micky stood in the doorway, his brow furrowed in concern.

"Izzy," he said, his English accent making my name sound sharper than usual. "Where in bloody hell have you been? It's been over a month since I last saw you."

I swallowed, my throat tight. "It's a long story," I murmured, my voice barely audible.

He raised an eyebrow, a hint of a smile tugging at the corner of his lips. "Well then, let's get to it. We've got all the time in the world, don't we? And if someone interrupts us, well—they can bugger off!" His voice lifted at the end, almost triumphant, as if he'd guessed what I was going to say. He opened the door wider. "Come in, love."

I followed him inside, the scent of incense and old wood wrapping around me like a comforting blanket.

It was quiet, too quiet, save for the faint ticking of an old clock on the wall. Its slow, methodical tock-tock-tock filled the room, a strange rhythm that made my skin crawl.

Micky led me to a small table in the back and started brewing a pot of coffee. "Now," he said, sitting down and fixing me with those sharp, almost unnerving blue eyes. "Tell me everything. Don't you leave a damn thing out."

I hesitated, wrapping my hands around the warm mug he set in front of me, struggling to find the words. "It's... it's Billy," I began slowly. "He's been trying to manipulate me. He says everyone is lying to me. He's making me doubt everything."

Micky smirked. "Sounds like he's the only one lying to you. I bet when you ask him questions, he avoids you like the plague."

Izzy stared at him, dumbfounded that Micky already seemed to know.

His brow furrowed, and he let out a slow breath. "You know what I'm talking about, don't you?" His voice was sharper, louder, almost a declaration.

I looked up, startled. "Yes... yes, I do."

Micky leaned back in his chair, his face unreadable, though his eyes flickered with something—understanding, maybe. He nodded, his fingers tapping against the edge of the table.

"And the chanting," I continued, my voice shaking. "I keep hearing it out in the marsh. It's real, Micky. I'm not imagining it."

He leaned forward, eyes narrowing. "And what else, Izzy? I can feel it, something more. What haven't you told me yet?"

I closed my eyes for a moment, the memories flooding back. "Last night... I saw things. Terrible things. There was a girl, upstairs in the attic. She... she killed herself, right in front of me." My voice broke as I spoke the words. "And then I saw him. The clown. He murdered two men, and an old woman. I saw it happen. The blood. It was everywhere."

Micky's face darkened, and he shook his head slowly. "That's how it happened," he said, his voice lower now, almost a growl. "A long time ago. Billy LaBlanc painted his face like a clown and killed his brothers, Glen and Dale. Then he murdered his mother, Mary. And his sister, Sara—well, she shot herself. No one knows why. Maybe Billy made her do it. Maybe something else did. But it's all bloody connected."

My heart hammered in my chest. "Billy... you mean the clown's name was Billy?"

"Aye," Micky nodded, his voice harsh. "But here's the kicker, love—I don't know if your Billy is the same one. Could be an evil spirit tied to the LaBlanc family. Could be something worse, something living. Either way, you're in deep."

I felt the weight of his words sinking into my bones. The ticking of the clock seemed louder now, more insistent. I glanced at it, its hands moving so slowly, but the sound—*tock-tock-tock*—echoed through the shop, like a countdown I couldn't escape.

"I've been feeling sick, Micky," I added, my voice trembling. "I can't eat or sleep. My body hurts, especially my kidneys. I even went to the doctor, but he couldn't find anything wrong. Told me it was just stress."

Micky's expression shifted, more serious now.

I lowered my voice, barely a whisper. "Micky, I've felt something. Since I moved into that house, it's like there's something attached to me. Following me."

Micky stood abruptly, his chair scraping against the floor. He strode to a shelf filled with old relics, muttering under his breath. Without hesitation, he grabbed a small vial of holy water, uncorking it with a swift motion. He poured a few drops into his hands, rubbing them together like he was preparing for something big.

"It's more than just a feeling, Izzy," he said, his voice dropping. "An evil spirit's got its claws in you."

I flinched as he placed his hands on my head, his touch warm and firm. He muttered a prayer, words that seemed to hang in the air between us, heavy with meaning I couldn't fully grasp.

"You're safe now," he said, his voice gentler. "The Lord says you can go home. You're protected."

For the first time in weeks, I felt something—relief. It was fleeting, but real, like a break in the storm. Micky stepped back, his face serious again. "You're protected, but don't get too comfortable. The danger's far from over. Come back tomorrow. Tell me what you see."

"Ok, I will. Thank you, Micky." My voice trembled slightly as I spoke, still absorbing everything.

Micky gave me a nod, his expression softening just a touch. "Remember," he said, raising his finger for emphasis, "you still may see things, but you're protected now. Don't let it shake you."

That night, back at the house, I stood by the window, staring out at the marsh. The air was still, but the tension lingered, like the calm before a hurricane.

Then I saw it—the flicker of light in the marsh. Another fire, the flames licking up into the night sky. My heart stopped as I saw figures moving around it, their shadows long and distorted, performing some kind of ritual. The chanting was faint but unmistakable, carried on the wind, a low hum that chilled me to the core.

And then I saw him—the clown. His face was painted grotesquely, white with streaks of red, standing at the center of the ritual. My blood turned to ice.

But something else caught my eye, something that made my breath catch in my throat.

Trevor.

He was standing on the other side of the fire, his eyes wide with terror. He was alive. *Alive.* He didn't move, didn't speak, just stood there, staring at the clown with a fear I could feel in my bones.

And then I heard it—a voice, faint but clear, like a whisper carried on the wind. "Izzy..."

It was Trevor's voice. He was calling me.

I stumbled back from the window, my heart racing, my mind spinning. I had to get out. I had to run.

I bolted for the door, slamming it shut behind me and locking it, my hands trembling as I fumbled with the key. The air inside felt heavy again, oppressive, but different this time. The marsh no longer scared me. Micky had protected me from whatever evil lurked there.

But Trevor? Trevor was a different kind of danger.

And now, I wasn't sure what was worse—the evil in the marsh, or the man standing just beyond the fire.

~ 20 ~

ALLIGATOR ISLAND

I parked outside *Micky's Magical Things* again, the shop's sign creaking rhythmically in the soft breeze, like an ominous heartbeat. The darkness of the night still clung to the sky, casting an eerie, faint glow over the town. I sat in my car, gripping the steering wheel so tightly that my knuckles turned white. It wasn't the comforting quiet of a peaceful town—it was too still, like everything was holding its breath, waiting for something to happen.

I glanced at the clock on my dashboard: 4:30. It must have happened at 3:33 again—the time when the Marsh and the house come fully alive. The ritual, the whispers, the knocking... always at that exact moment. A shiver ran down my spine as I realized how often the same pattern played out, like clockwork. What was it about that time? Why did everything stir at 3:33? The thought tightened in my chest as I sat there, gripped by the eerie familiarity of it all.

Trevor. His face flashed in my mind again—those wide, terrified eyes from the other side of the marsh fire. I had seen him. I know I had. But how? The sheriff said he was dead, that an alligator had gotten him, but how could I believe that after what I'd seen?

The Marsh. It always smelled like something rotten, something old and decayed. That damp, suffocating stench followed me everywhere I went. I hadn't noticed it at first, but now it clung to everything—the air, my clothes, even my hair. No matter how many showers I took or how long I stayed away, the smell lingered, like a shadow I could never shake. It had become a part of me, a constant reminder of the Marsh's hold, and I could never get rid of it.

My mind raced. Was Billy just a figment of my imagination? Or was he something more? A ghost? A demon? Or maybe just a man who looked like the killer? My thoughts spiraled, each one darker than the last. I couldn't shake the feeling that Trevor was still out there somewhere, waiting for me. Watching. I didn't feel safe, not here, especially not there, not anywhere.

A sudden movement in my rearview mirror caught my eye—the Sheriff's car pulling up. I jumped out of mine, waving him down. He rolled down the window, his brow furrowed in concern, his expression lined with exhaustion.

"Sheriff," I said, breathless, "Trevor—he's alive. I saw him. He was in the marsh."

The Sheriff looked at me with that same pitying glance he'd given me last time, like he knew something I didn't. "Izzy," he started slowly, "we've been through this. There's no way he could've survived out there. I'll have my deputies check the marsh, but..." He trailed off, his voice heavy with doubt, just like before.

"I'll be at Micky's," I said, cutting him off. "Let me know if you find anything."

The Sheriff nodded, his expression skeptical but re-signed. He motioned for his deputies to follow, and they headed off toward the marsh. I watched their taillights disappear into the trees, the pit in my stomach growing heavier. I didn't believe for a second they would find any-thing—there were some things in this town no one could explain.

I turned and saw Micky standing at the entrance to his shop, his silhouette a dark shadow against the faint light of dawn. He waved me over with a slight smile, but the concern on his face was hard to miss.

"Come on, love," Micky called out, his voice lifting like it always did when he sensed something I didn't.

The shadows from the early morning stretched across the street like fingers reaching for me. I managed a weak smile and followed him inside.

Micky shut the door behind me, his movements slower than usual. He gestured toward the small table in the back, where we sat yesterday. "What happened?" he asked, his tone more serious now. He poured two cups of coffee, the steam swirling in the dim light like ghostly tendrils.

I took a seat, gripping the warm mug in my hands. "I saw him, Micky. I saw Trevor in the marsh. But I wasn't afraid of the marsh anymore. It's him. He's the one I'm afraid of."

Micky's eyes narrowed, and he leaned in slightly, his fingers tapping the table rhythmically, mirroring the ticking I couldn't shake. "You're telling me Trevor was out there?" His voice lifted, almost teasing but with a dark edge. "You sure it wasn't the marsh playing tricks on you, love?"

I shook my head, my voice trembling. "No, it was him. I know it."

Micky's lips pressed into a thin line. He stared at his coffee for a moment before standing abruptly, his chair scraping loudly against the wooden floor. "Well, if you're not scared of the marsh anymore, then that's something. But Trevor..." He trailed off, his eyes flicking toward the window as though expecting to see something outside. "We'll figure him out, love. For now, you need some breakfast. Come on, I'm starved."

He grabbed his coat, tossing it over his shoulder with a swift motion, and led me out the door without another word. Micky had his own way of dealing with things—through action, not talk. He was like a clock, ticking steadily forward, never stopping, no matter how bad things got.

We walked in silence to *Tanya's Crawfish Shack*, the small diner nestled on the edge of town. The sky had lightened slightly, but the clouds hung low, swollen and dark, heavy with the promise of rain. The marsh's scent seemed to cling to the air, sour and damp. As soon as we stepped inside, the familiar sounds of clinking dishes and low chatter filled the space. I spotted Gail and Patricia sitting in the corner, their eyes immediately locking onto us as we walked in.

"Well, well," Gail said with a wide grin, "look who it is. How's the new house coming along, Izzy?"

I stiffened, feeling Micky's presence beside me like a shield. "It's fine," I said quickly, trying to keep my voice steady. But the weight of her question pressed on me like a thousand pounds.

Patricia's eyes narrowed, studying me. "You sure? You don't look too fine, sweetheart."

Micky let out a short laugh, cutting through the tension like a knife. "Don't you worry about Izzy. The house is coming along just fine, isn't it, love?" His voice lifted again, louder this time, with that odd edge that dared them to argue.

Gail and Patricia exchanged glances, clearly not convinced but not willing to push further. "Well, let us know if you need anything," Gail said, though her tone suggested doubt.

We made our way to a booth near the back, the shadows of the diner's dim lighting making everything feel just a little too dark. The moment we sat down, the hairs on the back of my neck stood up. I turned and saw a woman standing in the doorway. Her eyes locked on me, her mouth twisting into a smile that made my skin crawl. I didn't know who she was, but something about her presence sent a chill through me.

"Who's that?" I whispered.

"Oh, bloody hell, love," Micky chuckled. "Don't let her get your knickers in a twist. That's Rosie Fontenot, the town outcast. She's harmless, just a bit barmy."

She cackled, her voice shrill and mocking, like a witch from a forgotten fairy tale. "He's going to get you, Izzy," she crooned. "You can't run forever."

Micky's expression darkened, his jaw tightening. "Bugger off, Rosie," he snapped, his voice sharp and full of warning. "You've caused enough trouble."

Rosie just laughed again, that same chilling sound, before disappearing back into the shadows outside.

After finishing breakfast, we left the diner and headed back to Micky's shop.

As I settled into a worn armchair, I turned to Micky, unable to hold back any longer. "While you were researching the land and that photograph, did you ever find any mention of the baby? What might have happened to it? The girl in the attic said her mom got it."

Micky sighed deeply, rubbing the back of his neck before responding. "The baby... it's hard to say for sure, but the most likely theory is grim. Some of the rituals practiced back then were dark—sacrifices were made. I reckon the baby was probably one of them. Sacrificed in one of those bloody worships."

He paused for a moment, his eyes distant, as though he was remembering something he'd rather forget. "I have a lot of old books about the history of Bayou Vista. This land was once a gathering place for all sorts of cults and secret societies. They believed the marsh was a gateway—some kind of conduit between this world and something darker. They would offer whatever they thought would open the gates—animals, possessions... and in the worst cases, even children. The deeper you look into the past of this town, the more unsettling it becomes. That's why most folks just don't look. They'd rather pretend the darkness isn't there, buried just beneath the surface. A town of secrets, and Devil's Marsh, in particular... it was the heart of it."

He leaned back in his chair, studying my reaction carefully before offering, "Would you like to take a look?"

"Yes," I replied, feeling my pulse quicken. I wasn't sure if it was excitement or fear, but I knew I needed to know more.

Micky nodded and stood, moving to one of the tall, dust-covered bookshelves that lined his shop. He pulled out an old, leather-bound book, its cover worn with age. "This one," he said, placing it gently on the table between us. "It contains accounts from some of the earliest settlers. Not everything's clear, but there are enough mentions of the marsh, and what they believed lurked there, to make your skin crawl."

I reached out, hesitating for just a moment before running my fingers over the rough leather. The smell of old parchment and ink hit me, and a shiver ran down my spine as Micky carefully opened the book.

I spent the entire day with Micky—we looked through some of his books, trying to find out everything we could about Devil's Marsh. Ancient texts, local legends, and faded newspaper clippings lay scattered across the table, each one adding another layer of mystery to the land I now call home. The deeper we dug, the darker the stories became—whispers of rituals, disappearances, and sacrifices.

There it was -virgins, young children, and babies. The weight of the words settled over me like a heavy fog. "Sacrificed? That's horrible," I whispered, my mind racing with the image of a child lost to some ancient, twisted ritual. My stomach turned as I stared at the pages in front of me, their yellowed edges filled with cryptic drawings and symbols I could barely comprehend.

Micky closed one of the larger books with a heavy sigh, rubbing his temple. "Devil's Marsh has always been a place of mystery and danger. It's no surprise people stayed away from it. There are accounts of strange lights, eerie sounds, and folks who wandered in and never came out again. But the mention of a child being sacrificed... that's unthinkable."

"Why would anyone sacrifice a baby or a child?" I asked, my voice barely above a whisper.

"Power," Micky said, his voice low and grave. "In those old rituals, the innocent were often seen as the most powerful offering. It was believed that such a sacrifice would bring the strongest connection to whatever dark forces they were worshiping. Twisted, yes, but in their minds, it was the ultimate devotion."

I shuddered at the thought, pushing one of the old books away as if it might come alive in my hands. "So the baby... you think it could have been part of one of those rituals?"

Micky nodded slowly, his expression grim. "It's possible. But whatever happened back then has cast a shadow over that place for generations. And now that you're living there, it seems like that shadow is creeping back into the present."

Before I could dwell on it further, the shop door creaked open, and the Sheriff stepped inside, removing his hat as he approached. "Izzy," he nodded in greeting before turning serious. "I went out to your house, looked around the marsh where you said you saw Trevor." He paused for a moment. "There were no footprints, nothing to indicate anyone had been around. Trevor... he was more than likely killed by an alligator when he had that accident. If he'd survived and stayed around that marsh, another alligator would've gotten to him by now. We saw three of them just while we were looking for tracks. That area is known as 'Alligator Island' to some of the older residents around here."

The sheriff's words were meant to be reassuring, but they only added to my growing discomfort. *If Trevor was dead, then what had I been hearing around the house? Those whispers... whispering my name, like he or someone was lurking just out of sight. And why did it feel like someone—something—was always watching me?*

After the sheriff left, I turned to Micky, biting my lip. "Do you think I should try to sell the house? Maybe I should go back to New Orleans... This place—it's too much."

Micky's face softened, but he shook his head gently. "I can't make that decision for you, love. This is your journey, and only you can decide what's best. But whatever you choose, know that you're not alone."

His words gave me little comfort, and the weight of my situation pressed down on me. "Before I go back home," I said quietly, "can you bless me again? For protection?"

Micky nodded and retrieved the holy water from a small wooden box. He poured a few drops into his hands, rubbing them together before placing his hands gently but firmly on my head. He muttered a prayer under his breath, the words soft and calming. As his hands rested on me, a wave of peace slowly washed over me, like a protective shield forming around me.

"The Lord says for you to go home, that you're safe," Micky said, his voice calm but firm.

I clung to those words as I left his shop, the weight of the blessing lingering on my skin like a shield. But the fear, the uncertainty—it wasn't so easily banished.

That night, as I lay in bed, the fear returned, clawing at my mind. I closed my eyes, and I was back in the attic. The girl sat in her rocking chair, crying, but something was different this time. The shadows on the walls moved with her, like they were alive. The clown appeared, his face painted and grotesque, but he didn't seem to notice me. He walked past me, his machete dripping blood, and out into the marsh, his footsteps heavy on the creaky floorboards.

For the first time, I felt invisible, like a spectator in my own nightmare. But the terror was still there, lurking, waiting for its moment. As the clown disappeared into the darkness of the marsh, I heard it—whispering. Faint, but there. A voice calling my name, carried on the wind, barely audible but unmistakable.

"Izzy..."

And I knew... it wasn't over.

~ 21 ~

THE HAUNTING OF 3:33

I woke suddenly to a loud, insistent banging on the front door. My heart raced as I shot up in bed, disoriented, the remnants of my dream slipping away into the shadows. The house was dead silent, but the banging continued, rattling the walls and echoing through the empty halls.

Who could be knocking at this hour?

I glanced at the clock on my bedside table: 3:33 a.m. Again. **Always 3:33.**

The pounding grew louder, more insistent. My breath caught in my throat as I crept toward the window, the floor cold beneath my feet. Peering through the curtains, I squinted into the darkness. The driveway was empty.

But the knocking didn't stop.

Remembering Micky's words—*You're protected, you're safe*—I forced myself to take a deep breath. *I'm protected,* I repeated, trying to convince myself it was true. I crept toward the door, my steps slow and tentative. My fingers hovered over the doorknob, hesitating. The air thickened around me, pressing in from all sides.

I cracked the door open, just enough to see—and suddenly it was kicked wide, the force sending me crashing into the wall.

A figure filled the doorway, his shadow stretching across the floor. Trevor. Or was it? My mind scrambled, breath caught in my throat. This couldn't be real.

"Bitch," he spat, his voice cold and venomous. "You thought you could hide from me?"

I stumbled backward, trying to push the door shut, but Trevor—or whatever this was—was stronger. He shoved it open, stepping inside. His presence filled the room, choking the air from my lungs.

"I told you," he growled, every word slicing deeper. "You couldn't live without me. You're weak. You're stupid. You're ugly. No one will ever want you."

Trevor's words were punches, each one cutting deeper. His eyes burned with hatred. Every step tightened the knot in my chest. My legs gave out, and I crumpled to the floor, his insults pressing down like a weight I couldn't escape.

"Please, Trevor," I whispered, barely audible. "Don't do this."

But he kept coming, fists clenched, face twisted in rage. "Look at you," he sneered. "Cowering like the pathetic little bitch you are. No wonder I had to beat some sense into you."

Tears streamed down my face as I pressed myself against the wall, trembling, paralyzed. His fist rose, ready to strike, but before it could fall—he flickered, like static on a broken screen.

And then, he was gone.

The room was still. Silent. As if he had never been there at all.

I gasped for breath, chest heaving, the walls spinning around me.

The pounding in my chest drowned out reason. It was impossible, but I knew what I'd seen. **Trevor was back.**

I stumbled to my feet, hands shaking. I had to get out. I grabbed my car keys and rushed outside, the cold night air biting at my skin. My fingers fumbled as I unlocked the door and slid into the driver's seat. But as soon as I sat down, I froze.

There, on the passenger seat, was the cameo necklace. The same one I had left inside the house. *How did it get here?*

A cold shiver ran down my spine, and I jammed the key into the ignition. Nothing. The engine sputtered and died. Panic surged through me. I tried again—still nothing.

Heart pounding, I bolted from the car and ran back inside, slamming the door behind me. My entire body trembled as I leaned against the door, trying to catch my breath.

I can't stay here. Not after what just happened.

I ran to the kitchen, heart hammering. My hands shook as I dialed Donna's number, nearly dropping the phone. The call went straight to voicemail.

"Donna, it's Izzy," I whispered, my voice barely steady. "I can't stay here anymore. Trevor—he's alive. I saw him. I'm leaving Bayou Vista. I'm going back to New Orleans. Please, call me. I need you."

I hung up, my mind spinning. My eyes drifted to the picture hanging near the stairs—the one with the hollowed eyes. My stomach twisted. The woman in the photo was wearing the cameo necklace. *That hadn't been there before.*

My heart pounded in my ears as I stood frozen, unable to comprehend what was happening.

Suddenly, a door slammed upstairs, the sharp sound cutting through the silence like a knife. My breath caught, and before I could react, I heard it—the faint cry of a baby.

I swallowed hard, my feet rooted to the floor. The crying grew louder, its wail cutting through the stillness, coming from the nursery.

No. I couldn't go up there. But my legs moved anyway, pulling me toward the stairs like something unseen was guiding me. The house was eerily silent except for the soft wail of the infant. Each step I took felt heavier, as if the air around me thickened with each breath.

I reached the nursery door, my hand shaking as I reached for the knob. The crying stopped abruptly, leaving behind a suffocating silence. My pulse pounded in my ears, drowning out any rational thought.

The room was empty.

The crib stood untouched in the corner, the mobile above it swaying slightly as if disturbed by a breeze that shouldn't have been there. A chill crawled up my spine, the eerie stillness pressing down on me like a heavy weight, suffocating the room.

Suddenly—footsteps creaked above me.

The attic.

I don't know what possessed me to go up there, but I did. My feet moved of their own accord, as if something else was controlling me. I climbed the narrow staircase, each step groaning beneath my weight. The attic door was ajar, a faint light spilling through the crack.

My heart raced as I reached the top. The air felt colder up here, stale. I pushed the door open fully, and that's when I saw them.

The girl, her face tear-streaked, sobbing quietly in the corner, and the woman with hollowed eyes—the same woman from the picture. They were arguing, their voices low but filled with tension.

"Give me the baby!" the old woman shrieked, her voice sharp and cold, cutting through the air like ice.

"No!" the girl cried, clutching something close to her chest. "You can't take him. I won't let you."

"I want to know who fathered that bastard!" the old woman screeched, her eyes blazing with fury, her face twisted with anger.

The girl shook her head violently, sobbing harder. "I can't tell you. I won't."

The old woman's hand shot out, slapping the girl across the face. The sharp sound echoed through the attic, making me flinch. The girl cried out, cradling her cheek, but the old woman wasn't done. She lunged at her, fists flying, her blows vicious and relentless.

"Stop!" I screamed, unable to watch any longer. My voice cracked, echoing through the cold space. "Stop!"

The old woman turned slowly, her hollow eyes locking onto mine. Her gaze was like ice, freezing me in place. "What did you say?" she hissed, her voice dripping with malice.

"Stop," I repeated, my voice shaking, barely able to force the word out.

The old woman sneered, her lips curling into a cruel smile. "You're no better than my slut daughter," she spat, her voice venomous. "Sleeping with every man you meet. No wonder Trevor beat you."

My blood ran cold. *How did she know about Trevor?*

"And you're a thief, too," she continued, stepping closer, her hand reaching for the necklace around her neck. "Trying to steal my necklace, weren't you?"

"No!" I cried, stumbling backward, the air around me growing thick, suffocating. "You can't hurt me."

"I wouldn't count on that," she hissed, her voice dark and menacing. Without warning, she lunged at me, her fingers curled into claws, her hollow eyes wide with rage.

I turned and ran, heart pounding in my chest. The attic door slammed shut behind me, as if the house itself was trapping me inside. I didn't stop until I reached the front door, throwing it open and bolting into the night. My feet hit the ground hard, but I didn't dare look back.

I reached my car, jamming the key into the ignition with trembling hands. This time, the engine roared to life. Relief surged through me, but it didn't last long. As I sped down the road, my breath coming in ragged gasps, my mind spinning from what I'd just seen, I caught sight of something in the rearview mirror.

Trevor. Standing at the edge of the road, watching me.

I didn't stop until I reached the Sheriff's office, bursting through the doors, my chest heaving, my heart still racing from what I'd just seen.

"Trevor's alive!" I shouted, drawing the attention of everyone in the room. Gail, Patricia, and Loretta turned to me, their eyes wide, concern etched on their faces.

Why are they here at this time of the morning? I thought, suddenly disoriented. *What time was it? After everything that had happened, it had to be close to 5:00 a.m. by now.*

But when I glanced down at my phone, expecting to see the early morning hour, my breath caught in my throat. It wasn't 5:00 a.m. at all. It was 10:00.

I stared at the screen, my mind racing. *How was that possible?*

The Sheriff stepped forward, his brow furrowed. "Izzy, calm down," he said, his voice low and steady. "What are you talking about?"

"I saw him," I said, my voice trembling, almost pleading. "Trevor. He was at my house. He's alive. You have to believe me."

The Sheriff sighed, shaking his head. "Izzy, we've been through this before. There's no way he could have survived."

"Please," I begged, my voice breaking. "You have to check. He's out there. I know he is."

After a long pause, the sheriff finally nodded. "Alright, I'll send someone to check. But Izzy, you need to calm down."

I left the Sheriff's office feeling no better than when I arrived. My next stop was Micky's. I couldn't handle this alone anymore.

When I told him what had happened, Micky's expression darkened. "I can cleanse the house," he said, his tone cautious. "But it's going to take some time. Some things... don't leave so easily."

I shook my head, feeling the exhaustion in every fiber of my being. "I'm selling it," I said, my voice flat. "I can't stay there anymore."

Micky nodded slowly, his gaze distant, like he was weighing something heavy. He was quiet for a moment, then asked, "Are you sure selling is the answer? Sometimes places like this... they don't let go just because you do."

I met his eyes, the weight of his words settling into my bones. "I have to, Micky. I don't care if I have to leave everything behind. I can't stay."

He studied me for a moment longer, then sighed. "I'll talk to Preacher John," he said, his voice softer now, almost reluctant. "Meet me at the shop tomorrow at nine. We'll take care of it—one way or another."

Before I could turn to leave, Micky's hand rested lightly on my arm. "Izzy... be careful tonight. Sometimes, when you try to run, they follow."

That night in the hotel, I kept every light on, telling myself I was finally safe. But no matter how many times I said it, the words felt empty. Hollow. My pulse still raced, and every shadow in the room felt too dark, too deep.

The TV played in the background, but I couldn't focus on it. My eyes kept drifting to the clock on the bedside table.

It's over, I told myself. *You're safe now.*

But when the clock blinked to life at **3:33 a.m.**, my breath caught in my throat.

Then came the knock at the door.

~ 22 ~

FOOTSTEPS IN THE SHADOWS

The knock came again, louder this time, rattling the door on its hinges. I jolted upright, my eyes glued to the clock on the nightstand: **3:33 AM**. Unease twisted in my stomach, heavy and cold. I wanted to move, to rip the door open and yell at whoever it was, but my legs wouldn't cooperate. My heart pounded, louder than the knock itself.

Suddenly, I heard a door creak open, and a woman's voice broke the silence. "What are you doing?" she asked, her tone playfully scolding.

A male voice responded, slurred and thick with humor. "I told you, you've got the wrong door!"

"Sorry," another woman giggled, tapping lightly on my door before they both burst into laughter. Their footsteps stumbled away down the hallway, echoing like something out of a nightmare.

"Damn drunks," I muttered, barely able to catch my breath. The fear that had gripped me faded into irritation. Yet, the air around me felt thick, charged with a tension I couldn't shake. My eyes flicked back to the clock—still **3:33**. It was like time had frozen.

Sleep was impossible after that. I spent the rest of the night tossing and turning, my mind too restless to settle. My body was damp with sweat, and my heart seemed to thud louder with each passing hour. I scrolled mindlessly through my phone, but nothing could distract me from the feeling that something was off—something I couldn't name. My thoughts kept drifting back to Micky—the man who had once filled me with unease when I first arrived in Bayou Vista. Now, he had become my anchor, my hero in the midst of all this madness. How had someone so mysterious and intimidating turned into the person I trusted most?

By morning, I was up and out the door before sunrise, heading to *Bayou Bliss*. I needed coffee—lots of it. The town was already stirring, the thick, humid air hanging like a blanket over the streets. My skin prickled with sweat in the oppressive air. When I reached the coffee shop, Brenda was behind the counter, her bright red apron tied tightly around her waist, her eyes lighting up when she saw me.

"Well, if it isn't Izzy," she greeted me with that big smile of hers. "I haven't seen you in a while. How are you doing, hun?"

I forced a smile, hoping it looked genuine. "A lot better now," I said, though the words tasted like a lie. "I decided to move back to New Orleans."

Brenda's smile faltered for a second, her eyes narrowing with concern. "I don't blame you. That marsh... it ain't right. You're smart to leave it behind."

I nodded, taking the three coffees she handed me. "I'm just ready for something normal again."

We chatted a little more, but her words clung to me like the humidity as I left. The marsh wasn't right. I knew that all too well now.

When I pulled up to *Micky's Magical Things*, Sheriff Johnson was already waiting outside, his arms crossed, eyes fixed on me with a look that made my stomach flip. My palms grew slick with sweat as I approached. He straightened when I got closer, his voice soft but serious.

"Izzy, I've been waiting to talk to you." He paused, glancing around the quiet street. "We found something near your place."

I stopped in my tracks, my heartbeat quickening. "What did you find?"

"Footprints," he said, his brow furrowed. "Around the marsh. They look fresh."

"Footprints? But... Trevor's dead. He's dead. You told me he was dead." My throat tightened, my head spun, and a cold sweat broke out on my skin. My heart slammed against my chest like it was trying to escape. Every breath felt like a struggle, the air growing heavier and thicker, choking me.

The Sheriff let out a heavy sigh, his expression grim, eyes clouded with uncertainty. "I know, Izzy, and I'm sorry. I don't have answers for you. But those prints... they're exactly where you said you saw Trevor. In fact, they're all over your property. All I can say is, it looks like someone's been watching your place."

I couldn't breathe. My legs wobbled, and I felt like the ground was tilting beneath me. *Watching me? But why?*

Micky stepped out of the shop just then, his presence as calm and solid as ever. He placed a hand on my shoulder, and the warmth of it helped ground me, but only barely.

"Izzy," Micky greeted me warmly, though concern clouded his eyes. "Don't worry, Sheriff, she's no longer staying at the house."

I nodded, wrapping my arms tightly around myself, trying to steady my shaking hands. "Yeah. I... I just can't stay there."

"That's good news," the Sheriff said, clapping Micky on the back. "It's about time someone talks some sense into her."

I wanted to ask more about the footprints, about what it all meant, but my voice felt caught in my throat, the fear too thick to speak. Micky, sensing my unease, placed his hand firmly on my shoulder again, a rare flicker of tension passing through his eyes before he spoke.

"Let's go inside," he said softly. "We have work to do."

I grabbed the tray of coffee from my car and followed Micky inside.

Micky's Magical Things smelled like it always did—sage, wood, and something faintly sweet, like old books and secrets. Preacher John was waiting for us inside, pacing nervously. His usual calm had been replaced by an anxious energy that made my own pulse quicken. Seeing him on edge only amplified the knot in my stomach, and my fingers trembled slightly as I handed over the coffees.

Before we began anything, Micky gathered us together in the center of the room. His eyes were closed, and he whispered a prayer under his breath—soft but powerful. I closed my eyes too, trying to draw in the warmth of his words, feeling it settle over me like a protective shield. Preacher John murmured along with him, but his voice trembled, barely masking his fear.

After the prayer, we gathered the equipment—surveillance cameras and motion detectors. Micky needed to set them up around my old house and along the marsh to figure out exactly what he was dealing with.

The drive to the house was suffocating. Silence hung between us, and every turn of the road seemed to stretch out, tightening the tension in the car. My hands shook as I gripped the steering wheel, the weight of the situation pressing down on me like a vise. When we arrived, the house loomed before me, darker and more menacing than I remembered. The air was thick with humidity, but there was something else—something colder beneath it.

As soon as we stepped out of the car, a sharp, icy wind whipped through the yard, sending chills down my spine. My breath caught in my throat as Micky glanced at Preacher John, his face solemn.

"You feel that?"

Preacher John nodded, his hands trembling as he gripped his Bible tighter. "It's colder than it should be. It's unnatural."

I opened the front door and stepped inside. Just as Micky reached the threshold, the door slammed shut in front of him, nearly taking his fingers with it. My pulse quickened, and I felt my chest tighten. It was as if the house itself was refusing to let him in.

We moved quickly, setting up cameras around the house and near the marsh. But as we worked, the air grew thicker, more oppressive, like the house was breathing down our necks. Strange noises echoed around us—a baby crying, soft and distant. My throat tightened again, and a metallic taste coated my tongue, making each swallow harder. I stopped several times, glancing over my shoulder, but there was nothing. My hands felt clammy, and my heart wouldn't stop racing.

Micky paused beside me, his expression grim. "You hear it too, don't you?"

I nodded, barely able to speak. "A baby... crying. But there's no one around."

Micky's eyes darkened, a shadow passing over his face. "It's a trick. The marsh... it plays with your mind."

As we continued working, Preacher John's nerves unraveled further. The air felt suffocating, pressing against my chest with an almost physical force. My skin prickled, and my breaths came shallow and fast.

As Preacher John positioned the last camera in the corner of the living room, a sudden crash made us all jump. Books flew off the shelf, hurtling toward him as if they had a mind of their own. He stumbled back, his face drained of color, eyes wide with shock as he stared at the scattered books.

"What the—" Preacher John's voice cracked, his wide eyes glued to the mess. He took a shaky step back. "This... this isn't normal. We need to leave. Now."

I moved closer to him, my heart pounding so hard it felt like it would burst from my chest. My hands were cold and slick with sweat. "It's just... the wind," I said, though the words felt hollow. I didn't believe it for a second.

"Nice try, Izzy," Preacher John muttered, his voice shaky, attempting a hint of humor to mask his fear. "Well, I'm ready to get out of here."

Micky stayed silent, his gaze fixed on the house, his expression unreadable. For the briefest moment, his jaw tightened, and I caught the faintest hint of worry before he composed himself. After a long pause, he finally spoke, his voice low and unsettling. "There's more to this place than you realize, Izzy."

Later, when we reviewed the footage back at the shop, the real horror began. The cameras near the marsh flickered, static hissing across the screen. Shadows moved in the trees—too fast, too fluid to be human. Figures darted in and out of the woods, their shapes distorted, almost like they were melting into the darkness. And then came the sounds—low, guttural chants that sent a shiver down my spine.

"What is this?" I asked, my voice barely audible, my hands shaking.

Micky leaned closer to the screen, his face pale, his voice hollow. "It's worse than I thought."

On the screen, a figure appeared—a shadowy silhouette standing at the edge of the marsh, its eyes glowing faintly in the darkness. It didn't move. It just watched.

A sickening dread settled over me, cold sweat trickling down my back as I realized it was watching *us*.

And then, without warning, the screen went black.

~ 23 ~

THE DEVIL'S HOUR

I couldn't sleep. Not after what I'd seen.

My mind replayed the footage over and over—the shadows, the glowing eyes, the grotesque figures moving through the marsh and around the house. It felt like reality had twisted, showing us things we weren't supposed to see. And then the screen had gone black, as if even the cameras were too afraid to witness more.

I left my hotel room before dawn, the air heavy and damp, sticking to my skin like a wet sheet. The darkness clung to everything outside, making the familiar drive to *Micky's Magical Things* feel longer, more oppressive. My fingers were numb around the steering wheel, but the anxiety in my chest had only intensified since the night before. My heart thudded with every beat, making my breathing feel shallow.

Micky was waiting for me when I pulled up, standing in the doorway of the shop. His face, usually calm, looked drawn and haggard, the weight of everything we were seeing finally cracking his stoic demeanor. He gave me a single nod as I approached, wordlessly acknowledging that today we'd face whatever came next.

Before we even stepped inside, Micky spoke, his voice low but steady. "We're going to find out what's really going on out there. And when we do, we'll put a stop to it." His words weren't a question or a suggestion—they were a statement. It was clear that he was in control, that whatever we were up against, Micky was going to be the one to lead us through it.

Inside, the scent of sage was stronger than usual, almost overwhelming. It was like Micky had tried to cleanse the shop, but couldn't quite rid it of the dark energy that seemed to cling to us after watching the footage. Preacher John was already seated, his Bible gripped tightly in his hands, knuckles white, his eyes fixed on the monitor in front of him.

"We need to see the rest," I said, my voice thin, barely concealing the tremble beneath it. My stomach churned, and I felt the weight of dread pressing down on my shoulders.

Micky nodded silently, his eyes clouded with something I couldn't quite place—fear, perhaps, or maybe something worse, a knowing dread that he didn't want to share. He clicked the play button, and the footage resumed, the marsh and house reappearing on the screen.

The camera was focused on the house, still and quiet, with only the faint rustle of the wind in the trees. And then the clock on the screen flicked to **3:33**.

It was like something had been unleashed.

The windows rattled violently, the doors seemed to shake on their hinges, and the house itself almost pulsed with a strange energy. My pulse quickened, a cold sweat forming on my palms. The air on the screen shimmered, distorting reality, as though something was trying to push its way through.

And then, the figures emerged.

It started with shadows—faint, flickering outlines that moved in and out of focus around the perimeter of the house. They didn't walk; they glided, slipping between the trees and the porch like phantoms trapped between two worlds. But then, as the clock struck **3:33**, something else stepped out from the marsh.

The clown.

My stomach dropped, my breath caught in my throat, and my muscles tensed, locking me in place. There it was again—the same grotesque figure from before, dressed in decaying dark clothes, his painted grin twisted into something far more menacing. My hands gripped the edge of the table, knuckles white as the terror surged through me. He moved slowly, deliberately, as though he knew he was being watched. As though he had done this countless times before.

Behind him, a fire blazed to life, illuminating the marsh with an eerie orange glow. And then... it appeared.

A demon-like creature.

It was massive, towering over the clown, its twisted, horned figure barely fitting within the frame of the camera. It moved like smoke, fluid and unnatural, its eyes burning with a malevolent fire. The clown approached it, bowing deeply as if in reverence, and the demon extended an arm, beckoning.

"Oh my God," I whispered, feeling bile rise in my throat. My heart pounded so hard it felt like it would break through my chest.

Micky leaned closer to the screen, his face pale. "That's not human," he said softly. "That's... something else."

The clown circled the fire, performing what looked like a ritualistic dance, his movements slow and deliberate. And then the demon bent forward, extending its arm toward the clown. The clown offered something in return—something dark, limp, and humanoid.

Preacher John was whispering prayers under his breath, his lips moving in time with the shifting shadows on the screen. But it wasn't enough. Whatever this was, it was beyond prayers.

Then the footage glitched.

The screen flickered, the image distorting, and when it settled, a new figure had appeared. An old woman, frail and hunched, standing just beyond the fire's light, her eyes locked on the house in the distance.

"Who... who is that?" I breathed, my voice barely a whisper. "That's not hollowed eyes."

"She's been there before," Micky said, his voice low. "I've seen her the last night on tape. In the woods."

The clown and the old woman didn't interact, but something about her felt even more wrong than the ritual. She wasn't part of it, yet her presence was undeniable—something older, something darker.

The next night, we sat in the same dim backroom at *Micky's*, eyes glued to the screen. The footage rolled forward, but it was different this time. The house itself seemed to wake up at **3:33**, the same time as the night before. The doors slammed shut on their own, the windows shuddered violently, and the whispers began—faint, barely audible at first, but growing louder as the seconds ticked by.

Micky's face tightened as we watched, his eyes narrowing at the flickering shadows on the screen. Preacher John clutched his Bible even tighter, his hands trembling.

And then, as we continued to watch, something new appeared in the footage.

A figure. Human-like.

It moved differently than the shadows—more solid, more real. It didn't flicker in and out of the darkness like the others. It paced back and forth near the edge of the woods, always facing the house. Its movements were slow, deliberate... familiar.

"T-Trevor?" I stammered, my voice barely holding together. My heart slammed against my ribs, and my throat tightened painfully. That silhouette, those broad shoulders... it looked too much like him. But it couldn't be. Trevor was dead. I thought he was dead.

But there it was. Pacing. Watching.

Micky's expression darkened.

By the third night, **3:33** had become a dreaded marker of time. Every night, like clockwork, the house came alive. The footage showed the same violent activity—doors slamming, windows rattling, eerie groans echoing from nowhere. But it was growing more intense, more hostile, with every passing night.

Micky had been researching non-stop, his face pale and drawn from lack of sleep. He slammed the book shut that night, his voice raspy from exhaustion.

"It's the time of the murder," he said, glancing at the footage. "That's when the original killing happened. **3:33**—the Devil's Hour. Everything that's happening now... it's all tied to that moment."

Preacher John crossed himself, but it didn't bring the comfort I needed. Instead, I felt more trapped than ever. The house, the marsh, the clown, the old woman... they were all bound together by something much darker than I could understand, something that was growing stronger every night.

"Izzy," Micky said, his voice low and firm. "Whatever's brewing out there in Devil's Marsh, it's not going to stop on its own. I'll have to be the one to end it, love. One way or another, this has to stop."

His eyes locked with mine, and for a brief moment, I saw the fear he was trying to hide. But behind it was determination—something that told me he wasn't about to run.

"I'm not running," I said, my voice trembling but resolute. "Not this time. I'm standing by you."

The clock hit **3:33**.

The house on the screen shook violently. The lights inside flickered, casting long, eerie shadows across the lawn. And then we saw it again. Trevor—or whatever it was—standing just outside the house, staring in through the windows, his head slightly tilted as though he was waiting for something.

I couldn't breathe. My palms were slick with sweat, and the room felt like it was closing in around me, the air thick and suffocating. Then the screen glitched.

The clown emerged again, his painted face now twisted into something even more grotesque. And behind him, the old woman stepped out of the woods, her frail frame moving with unnatural fluidity. They were closer now, closer to the house.

The door creaked open, slow and deliberate, as though it was inviting them in.

I gripped the edge of the table, my hands trembling violently. My heart raced, every muscle in my body screaming at me to look away, but I couldn't. I was frozen, paralyzed by the horror unfolding on the screen.

"Can you stop this, Micky?" Preacher John asked, his voice cracking, filled with the same fear coursing through me.

The question lingered in the air, heavy and unspoken by the rest of us. We were safe inside *Micky's Magical Things*, but the house, the marsh... it was like watching something inescapable, an evil creeping closer, no matter how far away we were.

I swallowed hard, my throat dry as sandpaper, and turned to Micky. His face was unreadable, but there was something different in his eyes this time—determination, control. He was the one in charge now, the weight of everything we had seen resting squarely on his shoulders.

Micky finally spoke, his voice calm but cutting through the tension like a blade. "Whatever's out there... we're going to drive it back. I've faced worse." His eyes flicked to the screen. "The marsh, the house—they're tied together. We'll break whatever holds them."

There wasn't a trace of doubt in his voice, no hesitation. He didn't need reassurance from us, because he didn't need it. He knew what had to be done, and he was going to be the one to do it.

The clock on the screen flicked to **3:34**.

My stomach twisted into knots, and then, without warning, the monitor went black. I froze, my breath catching in my throat, as the darkness seemed to bleed from the screen into the room.

~ 24 ~

THE SHADOW OF DEATH

I left the hotel early that morning, the cool damp air biting at my skin as I stepped into the quiet parking lot. My footsteps echoed in the stillness, but for the first time in days, I didn't feel like I was being watched. Since I left Devil's Marsh, I hadn't experienced any strange occurrences. 3:33 was just another time on the clock, and that sense of doom that used to cling to me was gone. It felt almost too good to be true.

The house had only been on the market for one day, and I already had a buyer offering the full asking price. I should have been elated. But something held me back. I couldn't sell it, not until I was sure. There was a nagging pull in my gut, a moral responsibility. I couldn't pass on that nightmare to someone else, knowing what was still there. Not until Micky had done what needed to be done.

The house in New Orleans that Donna had been pushing me to buy was waiting. The one I should've bought in the first place. That's where my life was supposed to go.

I kept telling myself that as I drove toward Micky's shop, the tension in my chest building with each mile.

When I arrived, Preacher John was already there, standing next to Micky as they loaded up the preacher's SUV. The sky above us was thick with clouds, the kind that makes you feel like something terrible is about to happen, but you can't put your finger on it.

"Well, Izzy, are you ready for this?" Micky's voice broke through my thoughts, low and calm, like he was asking if I was ready to go grab lunch, not face down whatever had been tormenting Devil's Marsh.

"I... I think so," I replied, my voice trembling slightly. "Are you sure we can do this?"

Micky gave me a reassuring look. "We have to. There's no turning back now."

We drove in silence, the weight of what was about to happen pressing down on us like a lead blanket. When we arrived at the house, Micky handed each of us a small pack of blessed salt. "Put this in your pockets. Don't lose it."

Preacher John hesitated before taking the salt, glancing at the house as though it might come alive at any second. "I've seen evil before," he muttered, almost to himself. "But nothing like this. This place feels wrong... deep in my bones."

Micky moved like a man preparing for battle. As he rubbed his hands with holy water and placed them on top of our heads, I felt a strange warmth, a brief moment of calm. "God, I ask you to bless this vessel," he whispered. His touch was steady, but the seriousness in his eyes told me everything I needed to know. This wasn't just some cleansing. This was war.

Then, he went to the back of the SUV and began preparing himself. "You can't fight an evil spirit unclean," he explained. "Once I pray, don't touch me. It's like suiting up with armor. Touching me could put my life in jeopardy."

Preacher John swallowed hard and crossed himself. "Lord, give us strength."

I felt a shiver run down my spine as Micky poured water over his hands and washed his face, praying for forgiveness and protection. When he stepped back out from behind the SUV, I barely recognized him. His eyes were sharp, focused. His whole demeanor had changed. This wasn't the Micky I knew—the kind ole gypsy boy who ran a shop full of trinkets and curiosities. This was someone else. Someone fierce, someone ready to confront evil.

He carried a book, *The Prayers of Exorcism*, in one hand as we started toward the house. His voice rose in a steady chant, Psalms 23, "Yea, though I walk through the valley of the shadow of death, I will fear no evil. For you are with me."

We stopped at the porch, the side facing the marsh, and Micky bent down, grabbing a handful of dirt. "To sanctify the land," he muttered under his breath, scattering the dirt across the ground like a soldier setting up his defenses.

As we stepped onto the porch, Micky paused, placing his hand on the doorframe. "Lord, I'm entering a place of darkness. Bless me."

The house groaned, a low, rumbling sound that felt alive. Like it was waiting for us. The walls seemed to shudder, as though they knew what was coming. And the air—thick, suffocating—felt like it was closing in, pressing against my lungs.

What am I doing? The thought rattled through my mind. I could feel the weight of the house pressing down on us, as if it wanted to swallow us whole. *This is insane. How can Micky—how can any of us—fight something like this?*

Micky opened his book and began reciting the prayers, his voice strong but distant, as if the very air was trying to swallow his words. Then, without warning, things started flying. A book shot across the room, slamming into the wall. A chair tipped over and skidded across the floor, its legs scraping the wood with a screech. A picture frame smashed against the wall, glass shattering at our feet.

The house was furious.

The groaning grew louder, so loud it was all I could hear. I could see Micky's lips moving, shouting the prayers, but the sound of his voice was drowned out by the house's rage. The walls trembled violently, and the floor—it felt like it was moving beneath us, like we were standing on a conveyor belt, walking but getting nowhere.

"What the hell is happening?" Preacher John shouted over the noise, his voice shaky.

"It's fighting us," Micky replied, his voice strained. "Stay close."

We pushed forward, forcing our way up the stairs, the ground shifting under our feet. The air was thick, so thick I could barely breathe. My chest tightened with every step, and the walls seemed to close in, vibrating with an energy that was more than just noise. It was suffocating, like being submerged in something dark and malevolent.

I'm drowning in this house. I'm going to suffocate. My thoughts spiraled, panic creeping in as the air pressed against me. *We shouldn't have come here. We'll never make it out.*

When we reached the attic, I saw her—the young girl. She was sitting in the chair, her face twisted in a stupid, mocking grin, her eyes empty.

Before I could even react, she flew out of the chair, hurling herself toward Micky. He raised his hands, his mouth moving in a command I couldn't hear over the deafening noise. She disappeared mid-air, vanishing like smoke.

I wasn't ready for this. She looked so real...but she's not. She can't be. None of this is real. How is Micky doing this?

I stood there, heart pounding, sweat dripping down my back. Preacher John muttered a prayer under his breath, his face pale.

"Keep moving," Micky said, his voice like steel.

We moved down the stairs, the house groaning, shaking, as if it would collapse at any moment. As we entered Hollow Eyes' bedroom, a horrid laugh echoed through the air, louder than anything I had ever heard. It rattled my bones. Micky shouted something, and the laugh was cut off, silenced as if it had never been.

Preacher John stumbled backward, pressing his back against the wall. "This... this is madness. It's too strong."

"It's not stronger than faith," Micky snapped, his eyes blazing with determination. "We keep going."

We continued through the house, entering each room. I saw spirits—spirits I had never seen before—lurking in the corners, crawling on the ceiling. Some hovered in the doorways, watching us with hollow, dead eyes. One by one, Micky banished them, his voice strong, his prayers cutting through the noise. But there was no sign of the baby. No sign of the one thing that had haunted me from the start.

Finally, when we reached the bottom of the stairs, he appeared.

The clown.

His face was streaked with dirt, the grin on his lips widening as he laughed, a cold, terrible sound. He stood there, toying with Micky, like it was all a game. The house roared around us, the walls vibrating with fury. It looked like the wind was howling inside, blowing against Micky with all its strength, pushing him back. But Micky didn't move. He stood his ground, his feet planted firm, shouting over the chaos.

"Look at you," the clown sneered, his voice low and grating, echoing through the room. "You think you can save them? You think you can save yourself?"

Micky's eyes narrowed, his voice rising above the storm. "I walk with the Lord. You cannot stand in His way."

The clown's laugh cut through the air, high-pitched and piercing, making my skin crawl. He tilted his head, eyes narrowing. "I've been watching you, Micky," he hissed, stepping closer, his voice dripping with malice. "Ever since you were a young lad in the boys' home... I've been there. Watching. Waiting."

Micky's face paled slightly, but his voice remained steady. "I'm not afraid of you."

Boys' home? How does the clown know that? What is this thing? My mind raced.

The clown grinned wider, leaning forward as if he could sense my thoughts. "You think this is about faith, Micky? You'll need more than faith to save her."

Preacher John and I stood frozen at the bottom of the stairs, wide-eyed, our hands over our ears as the groaning, the screaming, and the laughter grew louder, louder than anything I had ever heard. It felt like the noise was going to burst my eardrums, crush my skull.

Things flew toward Micky—books, lamps, shards of glass—all missing him by inches, as though the house itself was trying to fight him. I wanted to scream, to run, but my feet wouldn't move. The fear was paralyzing, all-consuming.

Micky stepped toward the clown, his voice rising above the chaos. The clown let out a high-pitched screech, the sound piercing through the air. I closed my eyes, cowering against the stairs, and then, just as suddenly as it had begun, it stopped.

Silence.

I opened my eyes, and there stood Micky, drenched in sweat, his face pale, but his eyes sharp and alive.

"It's gone," he said, his voice barely above a whisper. "The evil is gone."

The house felt different. The air, once thick and suffocating, was light. The oppressive weight had lifted, and for the first time, the house felt... at peace. I took a deep breath, my legs shaking beneath me.

It was over.

Or at least, I hoped it was.

~ 25 ~

FAREWELL AT TANYA'S

Despite the peace that Micky had brought to Devil's Marsh, a deep unease still curled within me, like the shadows of the marsh weren't entirely gone. The house felt lighter, sure, and the buyer who swooped in didn't care about the history or the horrors. But I couldn't shake the feeling that some things never leave. They just wait in the dark.

Bayou Vista had become a part of me, and as much as I wanted to leave, a part of me still felt anchored here. I told myself I was just waiting for the paperwork to be finalized, but deep down, I knew it was more than that. I could have left this morning but I was lingering, haunted by memories—by ghosts.

Billy—who was the man I met on the road? The one who swept into my life with a smile that seemed to know all my secrets? The one who promised me peace, who held my hand at the lake and whispered he loved me? I felt so connected to him, like he was the reason I came to Devil's Marsh in the first place, like it was all meant to be. But when I was at my lowest—tired, confused, vulnerable—he vanished, like smoke in the wind. Is that all he wanted? To draw me in, to see how close I'd let him, only to disappear when I needed him most?

I still ask myself: Was he real, or was he something else? A spirit, a ghost of the marsh itself, clinging to me like the mist? He felt real. His touch, his words, the way he looked at me—all of it was real. Did I fall in love with a man, or was it his shadow, doomed to roam the marsh forever?

And Trevor... is he still alive, or did the marsh swallow him whole and leave only his darkness behind?

And Micky.

He had been my anchor through the madness. The strange, mysterious man who I had once feared was now the only person in this town who truly understood what I had been through. He wasn't just a friend. He was a hero. My hero.

Everything was set for the movers to arrive first thing in the morning, thanks to Cindy, the owner of *Burning Love*. She was the only one brave enough to venture out to the marsh and help me pack. Even though the house feels different now, with a lighter aura since Micky's blessing, I still don't feel comfortable staying here, so I'm spending another night at that cheap hotel in Crystal Cove.

If things had been different, I think Cindy and I would've become best friends. We have a lot in common, and she reminds me so much of Donna. There's something about her—strong, fearless, like she's seen the darkness but doesn't let it touch her. On my way back to the hotel, I made a stop at Micky's, carrying Mary LaBlanc's journal and a few old, dusty books I'd uncovered while packing.

"Hi, Micky," I said as I stepped inside.

"Hello, love," he greeted me with his familiar warmth, his eyes twinkling. "What do you have there?"

"Just a few things I thought you might find interesting," I said, passing him the journal. "Mary LaBlanc's notes... and a couple of other old books I dug up."

His expression shifted ever so slightly as he took the journal, flipping through the fragile pages. "Well now, this is a treasure," he said, his tone softening with reverence.

After a moment, he looked back up at me. "Fancy grabbing some dinner?"

There was something in his eyes—a spark of mischief, maybe—but I was too tired to question it. After everything, I needed something normal, something comforting. Crawfish, laughter, and Micky's dry wit seemed like the perfect way to ease the weight still pressing down on me.

"Sure," I replied, managing a smile. "Tanya's Crawfish Kitchen?"

"Of course. What else would it be?" he said with a chuckle.

And just like that, I felt the heaviness lift, even if only for a little while. Dinner with Micky was exactly the slice of normal I needed before facing the next chapter of whatever came next.

As we pulled up to Tanya's, something felt... different. The air around the place buzzed, like there was something waiting inside. I followed Micky up the steps, my hand on the door handle, heart racing for no reason. *Get a grip, Izzy*, I told myself. *It's just dinner.*

But when we stepped inside, I froze.

The place was packed. Tables were pushed together, and the entire town seemed to be there, filling the space with warmth and chatter. Preacher John stood at the center, his hands clasped in front of him, and beside him were familiar faces. Cindy and Dondi, laughing together. Shannon, Catrina, and LaDonna, whispering with bright eyes. Brenda, with her signature smile, standing close to the bar. And there, near the back, were the Sheriff and the Mayor, alongside Lena, Jason, and Firecracker.

I blinked, not understanding. What was all of this?

Preacher John's voice rang out, clear and commanding. "A job well done, Micky!" He raised his arms. "We've all come to say thank you—for what you've done for this town. You've rid us of the darkness that had settled over Devil's Marsh."

Everyone's eyes turned toward Micky, and I could feel the emotion in the room shift. Gratitude. Relief. Joy. They weren't here for me—they were here for him.

My throat tightened as I realized how much these people had been affected by the evil that had lingered in the marsh. The rumors. The fear. The way everyone had whispered about what might be hiding in the shadows, never daring to confront it until Micky had stepped forward.

"Let's hear it for Micky!" someone shouted—Taylor or Laurie, I couldn't tell—and a cheer erupted from the room. The sound filled the space, and I found myself caught up in it, clapping alongside everyone else.

Micky, ever humble, just smiled softly and waved, his rich English accent cutting through the noise. "You're too kind, all of you. But it was a team effort."

I stepped closer to him, watching as he accepted the praise with his usual grace. His presence was magnetic—people couldn't help but be drawn to him. Cindy Blevins hugged him, and even Melissa and Matilda—two of the town's toughest critics—offered their thanks. Gail, Margie, and Patricia stood nearby, beaming, and Loretta, Jill, and Tricia waved at me from across the room.

Mary and Tina, from the beauty shop, approached him last. Tina's voice cracked as she spoke. "We can sleep easy now, Micky. You did something none of us could."

I swallowed hard, the weight of their words settling in my chest. For so long, Bayou Vista had been a place where fear lurked behind every smile, and people were too scared to confront what they didn't understand. Micky had changed that.

As I stood there, surrounded by the people who had welcomed me in despite my outsider status, I realized that Micky had done more than just banish the evil from Devil's Marsh. He had brought hope back to this town.

But for me, the peace wasn't as simple. The shadows still clung to me, whispering in the back of my mind. Maybe they always would.

"You've become quite the local legend," I said, trying to keep my voice light, but the emotions behind it weighed me down.

Micky chuckled, running a hand through his hair. "I'm not sure about that, but it's nice to see everyone happy for once."

I nodded, biting my lip. "You've done something incredible, Micky. Something real."

He tilted his head, studying me. "And yet, something's still troubling you, isn't it?"

I hesitated, looking down at my hands. "I don't know. Maybe it's just... everything. The house is sold, but it feels like there's unfinished business. I can't shake the feeling that something's still there, waiting."

Micky's expression softened, but his voice remained firm. "You've been through more than most people could bear, Izzy. It's natural to feel unsettled after everything you've faced."

"I thought leaving would fix it," I admitted. "But now, I'm not sure. I keep thinking about what happened in the marsh, about the house. About that clown. I feel like I should be at peace, but..."

Before Micky could respond, the door to the diner creaked open. Rosie Fontenot walked in, and the air shifted. It wasn't just that the room had grown quiet—the very atmosphere changed, thickening like the humidity before a storm. The laughter and warmth that had filled Tanya's Crawfish Kitchen seemed to drain away, leaving only a heavy, suffocating coldness in its wake.

I felt it in my bones first, a sudden chill that crawled up my spine, making the hair on the back of my neck stand on end. The chatter around me dulled, like the world had been placed underwater, and all I could hear was my own heartbeat, thudding in my ears.

I tried to steady my breath, but it came in short, shallow gasps. My hands trembled, my fingers cold as though the temperature had dropped twenty degrees in an instant. I clenched them into fists, willing myself to focus, to push away the rising fear. But I couldn't shake the feeling that something—something dark—was closing in.

And then, Rosie's gaze found mine.

She didn't speak right away. She didn't have to. The malice in her eyes said enough. Her lips curled into a smug grin as she slowly made her way through the room, her presence sucking what little warmth was left out of the air. The room seemed to shift, the edges of my vision blurring as if everything had become slightly distorted. The familiar faces of the townspeople around me—Cindy, Brenda, Shannon—felt distant, like they were part of another world entirely. All that mattered now was the growing weight of Rosie's presence and the venomous look in her eyes.

"Well, isn't this sweet," she drawled, her voice sharp enough to cut through the thick silence. "A little celebration for the town's hero."

Her words were dripping with sarcasm, but she wasn't looking at Micky. She was staring straight at me, her expression darkening with every step she took closer. My breath caught in my throat, and for a moment, the room seemed to tilt. I gripped the edge of the table, my pulse racing as Rosie came to a stop just feet from where I sat.

"You think it's over, don't you?" she hissed, leaning in so close I could feel the heat of her breath against my skin. But even her breath felt cold.

The shadows of Devil's Marsh seemed to creep back into my mind. My vision narrowed, tunneling as the walls of the diner pressed in around me.

"He's still out there, you know," she continued, her voice sharp, like nails on a chalkboard. "The killer. The one you all think is gone."

My heart stuttered, and I tried to pull back, but it was like I was glued to the spot. Rosie leaned even closer, her breath a harsh whisper in my ear. "He's still coming for you, Izzy. Don't think you're safe just because Micky chased away a few ghosts."

Her words felt like poison, sinking deep into my veins. I wondered who she meant. Was she talking about Billy? Trevor? Could one of them be the killer she was referring to? The coldness in the room seemed to seep into my bones, wrapping around my lungs, making it impossible to breathe. I stiffened, my entire body locking up in fear. For a moment, I couldn't move, couldn't think. All I could feel was the ice settling in my chest, threatening to pull me under.

Micky's hand tightened on my arm, grounding me, but even his warmth felt distant, overshadowed by the weight of Rosie's presence.

"Oh, bloody hell, booger off, Rosie!" Micky's voice cut through the haze, sharp and tinged with his thickening English accent. He waved her off with a dismissive hand, but I could sense the underlying tension in his tone. Even he felt it—the darkness she brought with her.

And then, just like that, the tension broke.

The room erupted into laughter, the sound sudden and jarring. "Booger off, Rosie!" Brenda and Firecracker shouted from the bar, their voices high with amusement. Taylor and Laurie doubled over, clutching their sides, and the rest of the room followed suit, their laughter loud and bright, drowning out the chill.

But I couldn't shake it.

Rosie's eyes flashed with anger, her face twisting in rage as the room filled with laughter. "You can laugh now, fools," she spat, her voice venomous, "but you won't be laughing later. Mark my words."

She turned sharply on her heel, storming out of Tanya's with a final, ominous look over her shoulder. I watched her go, my breath catching in my throat as she disappeared through the door.

For a few moments, the room was silent. Her parting words hung in the air like a dark cloud, heavy and threatening. Then the laughter bubbled up again, people shaking their heads and dismissing Rosie's warnings as nothing more than the ramblings of a madwoman.

But the cold in my bones didn't leave. I couldn't shake the chill that had settled deep inside me. Despite the laughter, despite Micky's calming presence beside me, Rosie's words clung to my skin, gnawing at the edges of my mind.

"She's mad," Micky muttered, his smile returning as he tried to shake off the tension. But there was something in his eyes—something fleeting, a flicker of concern. He looked at me, his tone softening. "Pay her no mind. The marsh is cleansed. Whatever was there is gone."

I nodded, forcing a smile, but it felt hollow. I wanted to believe him—to trust that it was all finally behind me—but Rosie's words had sunk their claws into my mind, burrowing deep and refusing to let go.

"What do I do now?" I asked, my voice small, barely audible over the fading laughter.

Micky placed a hand on my shoulder, his touch warm against the lingering cold. "You live, Izzy. You move forward. You carry the memories, but you don't let them control you. You've already proven you're stronger than you know."

Before I could respond, Preacher John stepped forward, his voice booming across the room. "Izzy! A word?"

I turned, wiping my eyes quickly. "Yes, Preacher?"

He approached with his usual warm, commanding presence. "We will miss you, Izzy. You've become part of Bayou Vista, whether you realize it or not."

I felt a lump rise in my throat.

Everyone raised their glass, a wave of warmth spreading through the room. I looked around, taking in the faces that had somehow become my community—people who, despite everything, had welcomed me into their world. The lump in my throat grew as I realized how much I would miss them, this strange and haunted town that had woven itself into my life.

I raised my own glass, my hand trembling slightly, and forced a smile. "Thank you," I managed to say, my voice barely above a whisper. The room echoed with cheers and clinks of glasses, but even amidst the celebration, I couldn't shake the words that Rosie spoke from my mind.

The crowd began to thin, the laughter and voices fading into the background like distant memories. Micky and I stood together in the dim light, the warmth of the room slowly slipping away, leaving only the quiet echoes of the evening.

"I'm leaving tomorrow," I said quietly, not looking at Micky. The words felt hollow, like they belonged to someone else.

"I know," he replied, his voice gentle. "But that doesn't mean this is goodbye."

I looked up at him, confusion flickering in my eyes. "What do you mean?"

"Some ties are never broken," he said, a twinkle in his eye. "Even when the roads take us in different directions."

As we stepped outside into the night air, I felt the wind pick up, carrying with it a whisper—soft, barely audible, but enough to send a chill through me. The shadows outside seemed longer now, stretching out across the ground like they were reaching for me, like they hadn't quite let me go.

The road out of Bayou Vista was calling, but so was something else. Something that hadn't released its hold. As I stood there beside Micky, under the weight of the night sky, I realized with a sinking dread that maybe it never would.

And I wondered if I would ever truly leave Devil's Marsh.

~ 26 ~

NO WAY OUT!

I walked by the picture of Hollowed Eyes at the bottom of the stairs—Mary LaBlanc, the house's old resident whose gaze had haunted me since I'd first moved in. Today, though, she didn't look so scary. In fact, she almost seemed to be smiling, like she was silently telling me, *Good riddance.*

I smirked, shaking my head. "Goodbye, Mary. I'm glad I won't have to look at you anymore," I chuckled, feeling some of the tension in my chest loosen.

The movers were almost finished loading the truck, their heavy footsteps echoing as they hauled the last few boxes. Each thud reverberated through the empty house—a final reminder of the life I was leaving behind.

But as I stood in the doorway, staring at the hollow space that used to be my home, the air felt different. Lighter. The shadows that once clung to every corner seemed to have let go. Thanks to Micky, it felt as if the darkness wasn't as permanent, as if he'd somehow lifted the weight of the past.

Or so I thought.

Something held me back. A part of me lingered in the doorway, as if waiting for... something. The quiet pressed in, too loud in its emptiness. I glanced back at the picture of Mary. Her smile was still there, but now it felt more mocking.

Was she happy I was leaving? Or was she warning me?

I shook off the thought and turned toward my car. "You're free," I whispered to myself, hoping the words would convince me. But deep down, I knew the truth—the marsh always had a way of pulling you back in, no matter how hard you tried to escape.

I picked up my phone and dialed Donna's number, pressing it to my ear. She answered after the first ring.

"Hey! You all packed up?" Donna's voice was light, full of relief.

"Yeah, almost. The movers are loading the last of it now," I said, glancing out the window at the truck. I hesitated before adding, "I'm finally getting out of here."

"Good! It's about time. That place has been messing with you for too long. You'll feel better once you're away from Devil's Marsh." Her confidence was reassuring, but it didn't match the knot in my stomach.

"I hope so," I replied, trying to sound more certain than I felt. "It's weird, though. The house feels lighter, but... it's like something's still watching. Waiting."

"You're just overthinking it," Donna said, her voice firm. "It's just nerves. Once you're gone, you'll see it for what it is—a bad memory. Trust me."

"Yeah, maybe." I forced a smile. "I hope you're right."

"I am. You deserve a real fresh start. This time, it's for real."

I glanced around the kitchen one last time. "Thanks, Donna. I'll call you when I'm on the road."

"Alright. And don't look back."

"I won't."

I hung up, placing the phone on the counter. My fingers lingered over it for a moment. The room seemed to close in, the stillness thicker than before. Something felt... off.

Footsteps echoed behind me.

"We're heading out, Ms. Crown," one of the movers called. "We'll see you in New Orleans."

I nodded, grabbing my keys. One last look around the house. The quiet seemed to press harder, urging me to leave. My heart thudded in my chest, but I brushed it off. Just nerves. That's all.

I moved to the window, watching the movers drive away until the truck disappeared.

My phone buzzed on the counter—a weather alert. I sighed, tucking a loose strand of hair behind my ear. I needed to go before my imagination started running wild again. Before the marsh got inside my head.

I reached for my phone when a sound stopped me.

Footsteps. Behind me.

I froze, heart pounding. Slowly, I turned.

No one.

The doorway was empty, but I could feel it—something, someone—watching. A chill swept over me, colder than before.

"Billy?" I whispered, unsure if I wanted a response.

Silence. The room felt heavy, as though the air itself had thickened. My breath caught, and I backed toward the door.

Just as my fingers brushed the doorknob, a whisper came—so faint it might have been my imagination.

"You think you can leave?"

I spun, breath shallow, but the room was still empty. Nothing.

I shook off the chill crawling up my spine, forcing myself to move. My keys slipped from my hand, clattering to the floor. I crouched to pick them up, but something shifted at the edge of my vision.

I straightened, skin prickling, and backed toward the door. My hand fumbled for the knob, the cold metal slipping under my grasp. My pulse raced, my thoughts a blur.

Suddenly, the air thickened again, like a weight pressing down on my chest. I gasped for breath, vision swimming. It was as if the walls were closing in, suffocating me.

"Who's there?" My voice barely came out—a whisper, almost lost in the tension.

No answer. Just the sensation of eyes watching, waiting.

My legs trembled, but I forced myself to step forward. My hand finally wrapped around the doorknob, but before I could turn it, a force slammed into me.

I hit the floor, pain shooting up my side. Dazed, I blinked, struggling to clear my vision. Shadows danced in the corners, the room colder than ever. My heart raced as I tried to push myself up, but something heavy held me down, pressing on my chest.

"Please... stop," I gasped, voice barely a breath.

The weight didn't lift. It pressed harder, colder, until I could hardly breathe. My hands flailed, searching for something—anything—to fight back, but there was nothing but empty air.

A metallic scent flooded the room, sharp and damp, like the marsh after a storm. It overwhelmed my senses as the darkness crept closer.

And then, through the haze, I heard it—a laugh. Low, cruel, echoing through the room. The sound wrapped around me like a cold, invisible hand, squeezing the breath from my lungs.

The smile I'd glimpsed in the shadows seemed to hover above me, twisted and mocking. A voice whispered in my ear, close enough to feel the chill of it.

"You'll stay forever."

The weight grew heavier, crushing, until my vision blurred and darkness swallowed me whole.

~ 27 ~

BETWEEN THE VEIL

Micky sat in the quiet of his shop, *Micky's Magical Things,* surrounded by the familiar clutter of relics, books, and odd trinkets. His fingers drummed absently against the edge of the old leather-bound journal Izzy had given him. He hadn't had time to go through it yet, but something gnawed at him tonight—a persistent feeling that something was off.

He leaned back in his chair, the soft glow from a single lamp casting muted light across the room. His thoughts kept circling back to Izzy, to the strange sensation that had settled in his chest ever since she left the diner. It was almost as if the marsh itself had held its breath, waiting.

Micky glanced at the clock. She hadn't called since yesterday. Normally, he wouldn't worry—Izzy was independent and strong. But tonight felt different. Heavy.

He grabbed his phone, hesitating before dialing her number. It went straight to voicemail. His unease deepened.

"Odd," he muttered, setting the phone down, trying to push the tension away. Izzy never went anywhere without her phone.

His gut twisted tighter. He stood and began pacing around the shop, his mind wrestling with the growing fear. *She's fine,* he told himself, *probably got sidetracked.* But no matter how he framed it, the sense of dread refused to release its grip.

He grabbed his jacket. "I'll just check in, make sure she's out of there," he mumbled. "No need to jump to conclusions."

Yet the knot in his stomach knew otherwise.

The drive to Izzy's house was eerily quiet, the fog from the marsh rolling over the road like a creeping tide. Bayou Vista had always transformed at night, but tonight, the silence felt thicker, more oppressive. Micky had spent years living with the marsh's strange secrets, but tonight, that sense of foreboding clung to him like never before.

When he pulled into Izzy's driveway, the sight of her empty house struck him harder than expected. Her car was gone. The front door wasn't locked.

Micky pushed it open and stepped inside.

"Izzy?" His voice echoed, breaking the heavy silence. Nothing.

The house was still, unnervingly quiet, dimly lit by a single lamp in the living room. Empty boxes were scattered around, remnants of her move—a life in transition. His eyes fell on the kitchen counter—and there, next to the sink, was her phone.

He picked it up, his brow furrowing as he stared at the dark screen. Izzy never went anywhere without her phone. His unease sharpened into something colder.

"Izzy?" His voice was louder this time, as he moved through the house, but there was no answer. The emptiness was suffocating.

He stepped back outside, standing in the cool night air, eyes scanning the fog-covered marsh. His instincts told him to wait, to not overreact. But something was wrong, and he knew it.

He dialed Donna's number. After a few rings, she picked up, her voice groggy with sleep.

"Izzy?" she blurted, startled.

"No, it's Micky."

"Micky?" Her tone shifted from sleep to concern. "What's going on? Has something happened?"

"Has she shown up yet? Have you heard from Izzy today?" His voice was steady, though the concern was creeping in.

"No, not since yesterday. She was supposed to be here last night, but I wasn't worried—Izzy always gets sidetracked. Why? Is something wrong?"

Micky exhaled sharply, glancing back at the house. "Her car's gone. I found her phone here."

There was a long pause on the other end. "Her phone? Micky... what do you think happened?"

"I don't know," he admitted, his eyes shifting back to the marsh. "But when she gets to New Orleans, tell her to call me."

They exchanged a few more words before hanging up. The cold knot in his chest twisted tighter. Micky stood in the doorway for a long moment, staring out toward the marsh. He didn't want to jump to conclusions, but his thoughts were racing—none of them good.

Back in his truck, Micky's frustration mounted. There had to be something he was missing. His mind drifted back to the journal Izzy had given him, the one from Mary LaBlanc, the woman whose family had lived by the marsh for generations. If anyone knew the marsh's secrets, it was her.

But maybe this wasn't about the marsh. *What if Izzy was right?* A chilling thought crept into his mind—*What if Trevor was still alive?*

Izzy had mentioned it before, swearing she felt like someone was watching her, insisting that Trevor wasn't dead like everyone thought. Micky had dismissed it as paranoia, or stress, but now... What if Trevor had been lurking all along, waiting? He'd been abusive, dangerous. If he was still alive, and Izzy had crossed his path again...

The thought sent a chill down Micky's spine.

He sped back to his shop, his chest tightening with urgency. As soon as he stepped inside, he went straight to the journal. The old leather-bound book felt heavier in his hands than before, as if it held the weight of the past inside.

He flipped through the pages, scanning Mary LaBlanc's cramped handwriting, strange symbols, and cryptic notes. Her family had worshipped the dark forces in the marsh for generations, but there was something more—something darker.

He found the entry from June 1974, and his eyes froze on the words:

Something is very wrong with Billy. He's not my sweet boy anymore. He's been spending too much time out in the marsh. He keeps asking questions about his father, but how do I tell him the truth? That his father was a sacrifice. That the evil in the marsh has been feeding on us for years.

Billy's different now. His sister's terrified of him. She says she's seen him standing at the edge of the marsh, staring, like he's waiting for something. I've tried to protect him, but I'm afraid it's too late. The marsh has taken him.

And Billy... he's not Billy anymore.

Micky's hands shook as he read the words. Billy had been consumed by the darkness in the marsh. But what if Trevor had become something far worse?

He flipped through the journal again, searching for anything that could give him a clue, something that might point him in the right direction. The marsh had its evils, but the dread gnawing at him now felt more human. More dangerous.

Another entry caught his eye:

The marsh takes what it wants. And once it does, there's no coming back. But I fear Billy made a choice. He's become something else—something far worse than the marsh itself. The evil isn't just in the marsh anymore. It's in him. And it's spreading.

Micky closed the journal, his heart racing. If Trevor had somehow become part of that darkness—or worse, if he was still alive and had found Izzy—then he didn't have much time.

Micky took a deep breath, forcing himself to stay calm. There was no need to panic. Not yet. He wasn't going back out to the marsh—not with the camera already set up. If something had happened there, he'd know soon enough.

But it wasn't the marsh that worried him anymore. A far more unsettling thought gnawed at him—what if Izzy had been right all along? What if Trevor was still out there, waiting for his moment?

Micky clenched his fists, pushing back the rising panic. He couldn't jump to conclusions, not yet. But deep down, he knew this wasn't just about the marsh anymore.

Something—or someone—far more dangerous was lurking in Bayou Vista. And Micky feared that this time, the threat wasn't a place.

It was a person.

$$\sim 28 \sim$$

THE NEW FAMILY

The next morning dawned gray and heavy, as if the weight of Devil's Marsh itself had settled over the town. Micky leaned against the counter in his shop, his fingers drumming restlessly on the wood. He'd tried to distract himself, pouring over old books and the journal Izzy had left behind, but his thoughts kept returning to her. Her absence gnawed at him, a hole that couldn't be filled by reading or routine. The journal sat open on his desk, but his eyes drifted repeatedly to the phone—silent, no word from her. Nothing.

The small bell above the door jingled, breaking the stillness as Sheriff Emmett walked in. His boots scraped against the old floorboards, the sound familiar but weighted. Micky glanced up, meeting the sheriff's gaze.

"Morning, Micky," Emmett greeted, though his tone carried an edge of tension. He closed the door behind him, adjusting his hat.

Micky gave a curt nod. "Sheriff."

They exchanged a few perfunctory words about the weather, with a heaviness between them thicker than the fog that still clung to the marsh.

"So," Emmett said, pulling up a stool at the counter, "heard anything from Izzy yet?"

Micky's jaw tightened as his fingers halted their restless tapping. "No, Sheriff. She was supposed to check in when she got to New Orleans. She hasn't. No one's heard from her."

The sheriff frowned, his eyes narrowing into a concerned squint. "You think something's happened to her?"

Micky hesitated, running a hand over his unshaven face. "I don't know. But it's not like her to just disappear. She left her phone at the house. Her car's gone. Donna, her best friend, hasn't heard from her, either."

The sheriff leaned in slightly, lowering his voice. "You think there's a chance... Trevor could be involved?"

Micky's heart skipped a beat at the mention of that name. Trevor. No one ever found his body, though he was presumed dead. Now, with Izzy missing, the thought of him resurfaced, nagging at Micky in a way he couldn't shake.

"I don't know," Micky admitted, his voice quieter now, almost a whisper. "But she always believed he was still out there. She said she felt like someone was watching her... even before all this."

Emmett's expression darkened. "Do you believe he's alive?"

The question hung in the air, thick and suffocating. Micky had long dismissed the idea, had convinced himself it was just Izzy's trauma rearing its ugly head. But now, with her gone and no trace of her, the doubt gnawed at him like a ravenous beast.

"I don't know," Micky muttered, his voice barely audible. "But if he's alive... God help her."

The sheriff nodded grimly, his jaw set. "I'll keep an eye out, talk to a few people. If Trevor's alive, we need to know. And if he's got Izzy..." His voice trailed off, leaving the horror of the unspoken scenario hanging between them like a dark cloud.

"I'll be in touch," Emmett said, standing to leave. "If you hear anything, you call me. Immediately."

Micky watched him go, the tension in his chest refusing to ease. The sheriff had barely stepped out the door when Micky's phone buzzed. It was a message from Dondi. Something about a new family moving into the marsh.

Of all places, Micky thought, his stomach knotting at the news. Why the marsh?

He grabbed his keys, locked the shop, and headed to the *C&D Kwik Stop* to meet Dondi. The store was busier than usual, a few customers milling about the aisles, but the moment Micky walked in, he spotted the new family. A man with an arrogant swagger marched through the store as if he owned it, while his wife trailed behind, her shoulders slumped, eyes hollowed with exhaustion. Two wild boys, twins no older than four, tore through the aisles, knocking over displays and giggling like demons let loose.

The man barked orders at his wife, his voice rough and loud. "Get them in the car, Hannah! Now!"

Hannah, the mother, flinched but said nothing, grabbing the boys by their arms and trying to herd them toward the exit. The twins yanked free, disappearing down another aisle with shrieks of laughter.

"Damn kids," the man muttered, grabbing a six-pack of beer and slamming it on the counter. He looked at Dondi, eyes full of disdain. "You gonna ring this up or what?"

Dondi's expression remained calm, but his eyes flicked to Micky as he approached. "Sure thing," Dondi said, scanning the beers. "New in town?"

The man smirked, puffing out his chest. "Yeah, just moved into that old place by Devil's Marsh. Got a hell of a deal on it."

Micky's stomach twisted. "You're living in the marsh?" he asked, his voice tight.

The man, unimpressed, shot him a glare. "Yeah, you got a problem with that?"

Micky ignored his confrontational tone and glanced at the man's wife, who was now struggling to catch the twins. She looked like a ghost herself, her eyes glazed, her movements slow.

"You sure that's a good idea?" Micky pressed, keeping his voice level but unable to hide the concern lacing his words.

The man snorted. "It's a cheap place, close enough to work. Ain't no big deal. Just some old swamp, right?"

Dondi, behind the counter, glanced at Micky. "It's not just a swamp," he muttered.

"What was that?" The man's eyes snapped to Dondi, his lip curling in challenge.

"Nothing," Dondi replied evenly. "Just... people don't tend to stay there long. There's a reason it was so cheap."

The man barked a short laugh, shaking his head. "Superstitious nonsense. You locals believe too much in ghost stories. I'm not afraid of a swamp."

Micky felt the urge to push harder, but he knew it would be pointless. This man wouldn't listen. Arrogance had a way of blinding people to danger.

"Good luck with the marsh," Micky said quietly, his words tinged with warning. "You'll need it."

The man raised an eyebrow, clearly dismissing Micky as a fool. "Yeah, well, thanks for the advice, old man," he sneered, grabbing his beer and heading toward the door. "But I'll be fine."

The twins raced ahead, kicking over displays as they went. The man barked at them again, yanking one by the arm. Hannah lingered for a moment near the door, her eyes locking with Micky's. There was something in them—fear, maybe—but she quickly looked away and followed her family out the door.

Dondi shook his head as the door slammed shut. "Arrogant bastard. He doesn't know what he's in for."

Micky's jaw clenched. "No one ever does."

That evening, Micky sat alone in his shop, the journal open before him, but his thoughts were elsewhere. He couldn't shake the feeling of dread that had settled in his gut since Izzy's disappearance. And now, this new family in Devil's Marsh. The father's overconfidence, the mother's haunted look, the wild twins—it all unsettled him.

His phone buzzed again, jolting him from his thoughts. It was a message from Dondi.

Dondi: *Just heard from a regular. That new family in the marsh? They're already spooked—complaining about strange noises. Reckon it didn't take long.*

Micky's stomach tightened. It hadn't even been 24 hours, and the marsh was already making its presence known. He typed back a quick reply:

Micky: *Keep an eye on them. If they're hearing things already, it's only going to get worse.*

The night deepened, and a heavy silence fell over the town. But out in Devil's Marsh, something stirred. Something dark. Something patient.

And it was waiting.

~ 29 ~

EYES IN THE FOG

The next day, Bayou Vista was swallowed by a fog so dense it blurred the edges of the town. Micky sat at his usual table in the coffee shop, *Bayou Bliss*, but the familiar routine offered no comfort. Izzy still hadn't contacted anyone. She had vanished without a trace, and the weight of it settled heavily on him. Something had happened—something bad.

The journal lay open in front of him, its worn pages full of Mary LaBlanc's cryptic entries, but they remained just as puzzling as before. Each passing minute made the silence in the café feel more oppressive, like the fog creeping over the streets outside. His gaze shifted toward the window, where the world beyond was now a blur of gray. The air felt heavier than usual, and an odd sensation crawled over his skin. Why did it feel like someone was watching him? He hadn't noticed it before, but now it clung to him, an invisible presence that hovered just at the edge of his awareness, unsettling and unshakable.

As Micky took a sip of his coffee, the door to *Bayou Bliss* swung open, and a gust of damp air swept in along with the new family. They entered like they owned the place—at least, the man did. His wife trailed behind him, her shoulders hunched, eyes downcast, clutching her purse as if it were her only lifeline. The two boys raced past her, wild and reckless, their high-pitched laughter echoing against the quiet gloom of the café.

Micky felt his jaw tighten as he watched them. Something about the family unsettled him. The man exuded arrogance, his movements sharp and impatient, as if everything in the world was his to control. The wife, on the other hand, appeared to be slipping away, her spirit dimmed by years of whatever life she endured with him.

Brenda, the owner, smiled as always, her voice warm despite the cold energy the family brought with them. "What can I get you?" she asked, her tone steady, though Micky could see her watch the family with cautious eyes.

The man barely glanced at the menu. "Salted Caramel Cream Cold Brew," he barked, then scoffed. "Doubt this little backwoods place even knows how to make it," he added under his breath, turning to his wife with a smug grin. She hesitated before quietly saying, "Mocha Frappuccino, please."

As Brenda prepared the drinks, the boys turned their attention to a tray of freshly baked muffins sitting precariously on the edge of the counter. Before anyone could react, they lunged, sending the tray crashing to the floor.

Muffins scattered everywhere, and the boys stomped on them, their giggles rising like nails on a chalkboard.

The man's face flushed red with anger, and he turned to his wife. "What the hell, Hannah? Can't you control them?"

Micky's gaze shifted to Hannah. She flinched at his words, but didn't respond, her lips twitching as though she wanted to speak but thought better of it. The fear in her eyes was palpable, deeper than exhaustion—this was the kind of fear that left scars on the soul, the kind that stayed long after the bruises faded.

Brenda's voice cut through the tension like a knife. "Hey! That's enough." She pointed at the man, her eyes narrowed with authority. "You need to teach your boys some manners, and while you're at it, don't think for a second that you can walk into my shop and disrespect your wife or me."

The man's lip curled, but Brenda didn't back down. The weight in the room grew heavier as the other customers watched in uneasy silence. Micky chuckled quietly to himself. *He'll know better next time than to think he can walk over Brenda,* he thought.

The man barked at his kids to sit down, and they quickly obeyed, eyes wide. He paid for the drinks in silence, his jaw tight as he snatched them off the counter. The tension at their table was almost suffocating. After a moment, the man leaned toward his wife, his voice dripping with venom. "You look like shit. I'll drop you off at

Bayou Belle Beauty. Maybe they've got a miracle worker there, because I'm sick of looking at you."

Hannah's eyes flickered, a tiny spark of defiance that was quickly snuffed out by years of resignation. She nodded without a word, her hands trembling slightly as she lifted her cup.

The door jingled again, and in walked Gail and Patricia, their laughter light, momentarily lifting the gloom. They approached the new couple with smiles, but the moment soured as soon as they tried to introduce themselves.

"Hi there, I'm Gail, and this is Patricia. We thought we'd introduce ourselves—"

"Get away from me," the man snarled, cutting Gail off mid-sentence. His voice was cold, dripping with contempt. "I don't need to meet anyone from this backwater town."

Gail's smile faltered, but she wasn't one to back down easily. "Well, aren't you charming," she said, her voice laced with sarcasm. "You must be a real joy to live with."

Patricia, eyes wide with shock, whispered, "What a piece of work."

The man's jaw tightened, but it was his wife's reaction that caught Micky's attention. Her face reddened, a flush of shame and helplessness washing over her as Gail and Patricia exchanged looks and walked away, shaking their heads.

As the family left, one of the boys stuck his tongue out at Micky. Without hesitation, Micky stuck his tongue right back. The boy's eyes widened, and he tugged at his father's sleeve. "Dad! That man stuck his tongue out at me!"

The man turned to glare at Micky, but when their eyes met, something shifted. His bravado faltered. A flash of something passed over his face—recognition, maybe, or fear. Without a word, he dragged his family out the door, their footsteps echoing against the damp streets.

Later, at *Bayou Belle Beauty*, Hannah sat in the salon chair as Tina and Mary, the hairdressers, introduced themselves. "Welcome to Bayou Vista! I'm Tina, and this is Mary. What can we do for you today?" Tina asked, her voice bright but probing.

"Just a trim and a bit of color," Hannah replied quietly, her voice barely audible.

As Tina worked, she peppered Hannah with questions, her tone friendly but persistent. "So, where are you from? How do you like it here so far? Any kids?"

Hannah's responses were clipped, vague. She stared into the mirror, but her mind was clearly somewhere far away, retreating into a world no one else could reach. She wanted to say more—Tina could see it in the way her lips trembled, but something held her back. Fear, perhaps. Or worse, resignation.

When her husband arrived to pick her up, his scowl was immediate. "What the hell, Hannah? You look the same. Get a refund. You've wasted enough of my time."

Hannah's shoulders sagged under the weight of his words, but she didn't argue. She simply followed him out, her silence heavy with the weight of things left unsaid.

Their next stop was *Tanya's Crawfish*, a small local restaurant where the smell of fresh seafood usually filled the air with comfort. But today, even the scent of fried food couldn't mask the tension as the family walked in. The boys immediately began tearing through the restaurant, their laughter loud and disruptive. One of the servers, balancing a tray of food, was knocked off balance by one of the boys, sending plates crashing to the floor.

Tanya rushed over, her face tight with barely restrained anger. "I'm sorry, but you need to keep your boys under control," she said, her voice firm but polite.

The man's expression darkened. "Maybe you should teach your staff to watch where they're going," he snapped.

Tanya's eyes narrowed. "Or maybe you should learn how to parent your children," she shot back, her voice cold and sharp. "This is a restaurant, not a playground."

The man glared at her, his hands clenching into fists. "That's what's wrong with this town," he muttered to his wife. "The men are wimps, and the women don't know their place."

From a corner booth, Micky sat quietly, reading Mary LaBlanc's journal while he ate. The man's eyes landed on him, and his face twisted in recognition.

"Are you following me?" the man demanded, his voice loud enough to draw the attention of everyone in the restaurant.

Micky looked up from his book, his expression calm, his eyes glinting with amusement. "Bloody hell, I have better things to do than follow you," he said, his voice dry. "Now piss off."

The man's face flushed with anger, and for a moment, it looked like he was going to say something else, but the door swung open, and the Sheriff walked in, taking a seat across from Micky. His presence alone shifted the energy in the room.

"Is there a problem here?" the Sheriff asked, his voice low but filled with authority.

The man faltered, his bravado draining. Muttering something under his breath, he quickly gathered his family and left, his footsteps heavy with frustration.

Tanya walked over to Micky and the Sheriff, shaking her head. "Thanks, Sheriff. That man is something else."

The Sheriff rubbed his temples. "I think he's already gotten into it with half the town."

Micky nodded in agreement but kept his thoughts to himself. His mind was already drifting back to the journal, back to Izzy. He couldn't shake the feeling that something in Mary LaBlanc's writings connected to what was happening now. He just needed to find it.

The Sheriff leaned in, lowering his voice. "You found anything yet? Anything in that journal that might help with Izzy?"

Micky sighed, rubbing a hand across his face, the stubble rough beneath his fingers. "Not yet, but I came across something... unsettling." He flipped to the page that had been nagging at him.

"There's an entry here about Billy—Mary's son. His behavior with a girl from Crystal Cove. It's disturbing." Micky's eyes darkened as he began to read aloud:

Billy's eyes were darker today. I saw him with a girl—Sarah, from Crystal Cove. She was afraid of him, but he had a hold on her, a power. I don't know what he's capable of, but there's something dangerous in him. Something that could destroy us all. She wanted to leave, but Billy didn't let her. The air seemed to grow colder when they were together, as if it was feeding off the fear.

The Sheriff's face paled slightly. "Jesus... What was he doing with her?"

Micky shook his head. "It doesn't say, but whatever it was, it was enough to scare Mary. She wasn't a woman easily shaken, but the way she wrote about Billy—about how his eyes changed—there's something wrong there."

The Sheriff exhaled slowly, leaning back in his chair. "You think Billy did something to that girl? Maybe something's happening again?"

Micky's eyes flickered with doubt, but he couldn't shake the sense that the town was teetering on the edge of something much darker. "I don't know, but it's not over."

Later that night, back at his shop, Micky couldn't shake the feeling that something was wrong. The town had grown too quiet. He sat at his desk, the glow from his computer the only light, reviewing footage from the camera he'd left in the marsh. The day had been too still, like the calm before a storm.

As he fast-forwarded through the footage, a faint sound caught his attention. Footsteps. Slow, deliberate, crunching on the damp ground.

Micky leaned closer to the screen. In the corner of the frame, just beyond the camera's focus, something moved. A figure stood there, barely visible.

It wasn't walking. It was watching.

His breath caught as he paused the footage. The figure remained still, blurred, almost a mirage against the thick air. He rewound the tape, his fingers trembling slightly, but when he played it again, the figure had vanished.

He tried to tell himself it was nothing, just a trick of his mind, but deep down he knew better. Whatever it was... it wasn't a ghost. It was something worse. Something human.

Micky glanced up at the small security camera in the corner of his shop. The red light blinked steadily, reflecting his own distorted image back at him, as if mocking him.

And then, for the briefest of moments, he saw it again.

A figure.

Not on the screen this time, but outside his shop, staring in through the window.

Micky shot to his feet, his pulse racing, breath coming in short bursts.

But when he looked again, the figure was gone.

~ 30 ~

FACES IN THE CROWD

The town square bustled with life. Every year, Bayou Vista hosted its annual Fall Fest, a time when businesses lined the streets, setting up tables full of samples, deals, and coupons to draw in customers. It was one of those small-town traditions that brought out the entire community, but today, an undercurrent of unease crept through the air. Micky Vermooch sat at his table outside *Micky's Magical Things*, his eyes scanning the crowd for anything out of place. Ever since Izzy had vanished, he'd been on edge.

It wasn't just her disappearance—it was the figure he'd seen outside his shop.

He hadn't been able to shake the feeling that whoever—or whatever—it was had been watching him. Waiting. The thought gnawed at him now, sitting in the middle of the bustling Fall Fest, surrounded by cheerful faces but unable to let go of the chill that still clung to his bones.

But it wasn't just Izzy.

The new family had settled into the old house at the edge of Devil's Marsh. Since their arrival, strange incidents had already started to ripple through town, unsettling the tight-knit community. Micky couldn't shake the sense that they were somehow connected to something darker lurking beneath the surface.

He spotted them in the crowd—the man, his wife Hannah, and their twin boys. They were hard to miss. The twins had their faces painted like clowns, the white makeup cracking around their lips, bright red circles on their cheeks. Their father, towering and arrogant, led the way, cutting through the crowd as if the whole town owed him something. Hannah followed closely, her shoulders hunched, her eyes darting nervously, as though she expected a blow at any moment.

The festival should have been festive, but wherever this family went, tension followed.

The family made their rounds, stopping at each booth. Business owners, who'd already had run-ins with them, now braced for another.

Cindy and Dondi from *C&D Kwik Stop* were first. Cindy smiled, but it didn't reach her eyes. She shoved a bag of samples into Hannah's hands and sent them away with a curt, "Enjoy."

Tanya, from *Tanya's Crawfish*, turned pale when the boys approached her table. She barely spoke, dropping a coupon into their bag, her hand shaking as the father sneered down at her.

When the boys spotted LaDonna's table, stacked with delicate baked goods, Micky could almost sense what was coming.

The twins ran straight for the cookies.

"LaDonna, watch out!" Shanster from *Shanster Travels* across the street called, but it was too late. One of the boys grabbed a tray of cupcakes, knocking the entire table over in a crash of frosting and broken glass. LaDonna leapt to her feet, furious.

"You little monsters!" she shouted, hands trembling with anger as she pointed at the mess. The father stepped forward, towering over her.

"They're just kids," he growled. "Maybe if you had better control of your setup, this wouldn't happen."

LaDonna didn't back down. "Maybe if you had better control of your kids, my table wouldn't be destroyed!"

The tension was thick as a crowd began to form, watching the confrontation. Micky's heart raced. It wasn't the first time the family had caused trouble in town, but this felt different—more dangerous.

Catrina, from *Catrina's Closet*, stepped in. "She's right," she said, her voice firm. "You can't let them keep running wild like this."

The father's face flushed with anger, veins pulsing in his neck. He clenched his fists but said nothing, knowing the crowd wasn't on his side. Without another word, he grabbed his sons by the arms and yanked them away from LaDonna's destroyed table.

As they moved on, Lena from the library leaned closer to Cindy Blevins at the next booth, her voice low and urgent. "They came into the library yesterday," Lena whispered. "The boys pulled half the books off the shelves. Their father didn't even care."

Cindy scoffed, shaking her head. "They came into *Burning Love* yesterday too. Didn't buy a thing, just made a mess. The boys kept touching everything, like it was some kind of playground."

Lena's voice dropped even lower. "He didn't say a word, Cindy?"

"Just stood there, like... I don't know," Cindy grumbled.

"Something's wrong with him," Lena sighed.

Cindy's expression darkened. "They're nothing but trouble."

Brenda from *Bayou Bliss* caught sight of them approaching and, without missing a beat, waved them away from her table with a forced smile, avoiding any further trouble.

Micky watched as they made their way toward *Berry's Market* next. Taylor smiled warmly, as she always did, but the instant she noticed the twins' faces, her expression faltered. The clowns. She hesitated, unsure whether to engage.

"Why are their faces painted like clowns?" Taylor asked innocently.

The father's eyes narrowed, his voice dripping with hostility. "Mind your own damn business, lady."

Taylor flinched, retreating into silence as the family moved on. Micky's gut twisted when he realized they were headed in his direction.

When they reached his booth, Micky noticed something peculiar in the way the twins moved—like they were drawn to something. Their father, usually the first to barge in, stayed back, his posture rigid. He eyed Micky's table as though it repelled him.

Micky smiled, trying to keep his demeanor calm. "What's with the face paint, boys?"

Before the twins could answer, Hannah spoke up, her voice soft, almost apologetic. "Oh, their imaginary friend Billy told them to do it. You know how kids are."

One of the twins shot her a sharp look. "He's not imaginary!" the boy hollered, his voice high-pitched and insistent.

Micky's smile faltered, his pulse quickening. His eyes darted to Hannah, who giggled nervously, as if trying to brush it off. "Kids and their imaginations," she said, her voice trembling. But Micky saw it—the way her hands trembled, the slight glance she cast at her husband. She was scared.

Hannah tried to smile, but her face betrayed her. Every nerve in her body was telling her to run, to pull the boys away from the house and never look back. But how could she? He wouldn't let her. She could feel his eyes on her now, watching, waiting for her to slip up. Any hint of disobedience would only make things worse.

Then, the other twin spoke, his tone eerie, too serious for a child. "Billy says we'll never leave," he said matter-of-factly. "We'll stay forever."

A cold chill crept up Micky's spine. His hand twitched as he instinctively reached for the charm he kept around his wrist, a protective talisman he rarely had to rely on. His throat tightened, the words forming before he could stop himself. "Hannah, you need to listen to me."

She looked up, her eyes wide and startled. "What do you mean?"

Micky leaned in, his voice low but urgent. "I don't think Billy's imaginary. There's something wrong in that house. I think there's real danger in Devil's Marsh. A man, not a ghost. Someone... evil."

Her face paled, and she took a shaky step back. "I... I don't know how much longer we'll be staying. My husband says the house is a dump. We might leave soon."

"Hannah," Micky pressed, his voice softening, "this isn't about the house being a dump. You can feel it, can't you? Something is wrong. You and your kids need to leave."

Hannah bit her lip, her eyes darting nervously to the twins. She wanted to say something—to ask for help—but the weight of her husband's presence loomed like a shadow. "But... where would we go? He... he won't listen."

Micky leaned in closer. His heart raced. "You have to try. I think there's a killer out there. Not just in the house—out in the marsh. You have to leave, now."

Before Micky could continue, one of the twins piped up again. "Billy says we'll never leave."

Micky's chest tightened. He tried again, desperate to warn her. "Hannah, listen to me. You and your kids need to get out of there. I don't care what your husband says. There's a killer out there."

The father's voice suddenly cut through the air, sharp and furious. "What did you say?"

The towering man stormed over, his face a mask of fury. He grabbed Hannah's arm with a rough pull, yanking her back toward him.

"I'm warning her," Micky said, his voice steady, though inside his heart pounded like a drum. "There's something dangerous in that house, in the marsh. I think there's a murderer."

"We don't believe in your hocus-pocus bullshit," the father snapped, his grip tightening on Hannah's arm. His voice was low, menacing—like a predator catching the scent of fear.

Micky ignored him, his focus still on Hannah. "Please, take your kids and leave before something happens."

Hannah's gaze flickered with uncertainty, and for a split second, Micky thought she might break. He saw the fear in her eyes, saw her lips tremble as though she were about to speak.

But then her husband's voice cut through the air again, sharper this time, colder. "I said, mind your own business."

The father jerked Hannah back, his eyes flashing with anger as he dragged her away from the table. Micky watched helplessly as they walked off, Hannah's eyes pleading with him silently, her shoulders hunched under the weight of her husband's control.

Just as they disappeared into the crowd, Preacher John approached, his expression serious. "What's going on, Micky?"

Micky rubbed his face, trying to steady his thoughts. "It's the family. I tried to warn her, but that husband of hers..."

"Warn her about what?" Preacher John asked, his voice quiet but firm.

Micky sighed, his hands trembling slightly. "I haven't heard from Izzy. I've been reviewing footage from the marsh. There's something out there, John. It's not a spirit. It's a person. Someone dangerous."

Preacher John's brow furrowed, concern flashing across his face. "Footage? What kind of footage? Have you seen something?"

Micky hesitated, feeling the weight of the words he was about to speak. "I've seen someone. A figure. Out there, in the marsh. Watching. And... I thought I saw someone outside my shop last night, too."

Preacher John's expression tightened, doubt creeping into his voice. "Are you sure it's not just... paranoia? We've all been a bit on edge since Izzy went missing."

"I wish I could say it was," Micky said, his voice barely above a whisper. "But it's real, John. It's real. And if that family doesn't leave soon, I'm afraid they won't be the only ones in danger."

Preacher John fell silent, his face pale as he stared at Micky. The weight of what was unsaid hung between them.

They both knew something was coming—something that couldn't be stopped.

~ 31 ~

VANISHED

Days had passed, and no one in Bayou Vista had seen the family since the Fall Fest. The twins, with their unsettling clown-painted faces, were no longer causing chaos in town. The father's towering, arrogant presence and Hannah's trembling shadow were nowhere to be found. At first, no one thought much of it—people in town figured the newcomers were settling into their new home, possibly avoiding the town that had grown weary of their antics.

But soon, people started to talk.

Micky sat behind the counter at *Micky's Magical Things*, sipping coffee, his mind buzzing with the growing silence around Devil's Marsh. He hadn't seen the family since the day he'd warned Hannah about the danger. His gut twisted, an unshakable feeling of dread gnawing at him.

"Something's not right," Micky muttered, staring down at the cup in his hands. The weight of it all felt heavy on his chest. He had tried to warn Hannah, but now they were gone—vanished, as if the marsh had swallowed them whole.

The bell above the door chimed, and Brenda from *Bayou Bliss* walked in. "Morning, Micky," she said, her voice casual, but her eyes were watchful.

"Brenda." Micky forced a smile, though his thoughts were far from the small talk that usually filled their mornings.

She leaned on the counter, glancing around before speaking. "I haven't seen that new family in days. You think they skipped town already?"

Micky's throat tightened. He hesitated before answering. "I don't know. Haven't seen them since the festival. I've got a bad feeling about it."

Brenda's eyebrows lifted, her expression shifting from curiosity to concern. "What kind of bad feeling?"

Micky's voice lowered, filled with the weight of what he'd been carrying. "I've been reviewing footage from a camera I set up near the marsh. I saw something... strange."

Brenda leaned in. "Strange how?"

He swallowed hard, replaying the image of one of the twins in his mind. "I saw one of the twins. Just standing there, staring into the camera like he knew it was there. And there was something wrong with him... with his smile."

Brenda's face paled. "Micky, you think something's happened to them?"

"I don't know," Micky admitted, his frustration growing. "I told the sheriff, but there's no sign of foul play. It's like they've just... disappeared."

Brenda nodded, her usual cheerful demeanor replaced by unease. "If you hear anything, let me know, okay?"

Micky nodded, watching as she left the shop. The conversation hadn't eased the knot of anxiety in his chest. If anything, it made it worse. He sat back down and turned his attention to the footage again. He'd been glued to the screen for days, replaying it over and over, searching for answers.

The camera's feed flickered. Micky leaned in closer. There, in the background, a figure stood just beyond the marsh's edge, barely visible in the frame. His breath caught as he zoomed in, fingers trembling.

The figure began to move, stepping out from the trees.

Micky's stomach turned cold. The man's face came into focus—eyes locked on the camera, his lips curving into a grotesque smile that stretched unnaturally wide.

"Bloody hell..." Micky muttered under his breath. His hands were sweating as he paused the footage, his mind racing. A man stared into the lens, his features distorted with something sinister. *Could it possibly be... Trevor?*

The bell above the door chimed again, pulling Micky out of his trance. He nearly knocked over his cup as the Sheriff, Emmett, stepped inside, his face grim.

Micky looked up, shaking the lingering image of that terrifying smile. "Sheriff," he greeted, trying to keep his voice steady, "something wrong?"

Emmett rubbed the back of his neck, his expression troubled. "Got a call from Loretta. No one's seen that family in days. I went out to check their place—doors were locked, no sign of foul play." He lowered his voice. "But something doesn't feel right. The house... it feels off."

Micky stiffened. "Off how?"

Emmett shook his head, frustration clear on his face. "Can't put my finger on it. No signs of a struggle, no break-ins. Their car's still there. It's like they just vanished."

The Sheriff's words sent a chill through Micky. "I've been watching footage from the marsh," Micky said. "I saw a man, standing there, staring right into the camera like he knew it was watching him. It wasn't normal, Emmett."

The Sheriff's brow furrowed. "You sure it wasn't just a trick of the light? These cameras can play tricks on you."

"No," Micky said firmly. "This wasn't a trick. It was him. And there was something... off about him."

Emmett exhaled, his hand resting on the hilt of his gun. "Alright, I'll take another look. But listen, Micky, we can't start spreading panic. Half this town already thinks the marsh is cursed again. We don't need to fuel those rumors."

Micky's pulse quickened. "I know people are talking, Sheriff, but this is different. It's someone human out there."

Emmett paused, studying Micky for a moment. "Did you save the image?"

"Yeah," Micky nodded, his gaze flicking back to the screen. "I was going to call Donna, see if she has a picture of Trevor."

"Trevor?" Emmett's voice grew sharper, his eyes narrowing with suspicion.

"Yeah," Micky said, his stomach knotting. "I think it might be him."

Emmett's face darkened. "Trevor..." The name hung in the air, heavy with memories and unspoken tension. "Let me know what Donna says, but keep this between us for now. We don't need the whole town panicking."

"I will," Micky agreed, though inside, unease twisted tighter in his chest. He knew something more was happening, but Emmett was right—spreading fear could make everything worse. "I'll keep watching the footage. If anything else comes up..."

"You call me," Emmett said firmly. "And don't do anything reckless, Micky. Let me handle it."

After the sheriff left, Micky sat back down, staring at the frozen image on his screen. That grotesque smile haunted him. The man's eyes were void of life, yet he was still moving, still watching. The dread gnawed at Micky's mind.

A few days later, Donna sent Micky a picture of Trevor. His heart pounded as he opened it, comparing the image to the face burned in his mind from the footage.

It wasn't him. Definitely not Trevor.

Micky felt a strange mix of relief and frustration. He had been so sure, but now he was back at square one. The dread remained, lurking just beneath the surface.

That night, Micky tossed and turned in his bed, unable to sleep. When he finally drifted off, the nightmare hit him like a freight train.

In the dream, Micky was back at the shop, reviewing the footage once more. The air around him felt thick and suffocating. He clicked through the frames, his heart pounding.

There it was—a figure.

His breath caught as he zoomed in. It was one of the twins. The boy's face was smeared with clown makeup, his movements jerky, unnatural. The boy's lips began to move, mouthing something Micky couldn't quite hear.

"Billy... Billy..."

Micky felt a sickening twist in his gut. The boy's smile was too wide, too wrong—stretching unnaturally across his face. It wasn't just a child's smile. It was something darker, something inhuman.

The boy moved closer to the marsh, his body stiff, as though being pulled by invisible strings. "Billy says we'll never leave," the boy whispered, his voice distorted, warped like something out of a nightmare.

The boy took one final step and vanished into the marsh.

Micky jolted awake, drenched in sweat, his heart pounding in his chest. He sat up, gasping for breath, the nightmare still vivid in his mind. It had felt so real—the boy's smile, the laughter, the way the marsh seemed to pull him in—it gnawed at his sanity.

He reached for his phone, but then stopped. The words from the dream echoed in his mind, the boy's voice a haunting whisper. "Billy says we'll never leave."

Micky returned to the shop early the next morning, the remnants of the nightmare still clinging to his thoughts. He couldn't shake the feeling that something was wrong—more than wrong. Urgency twisted inside him, mixing with fear as he sat down at his desk, pulling up the footage from the marsh yet again.

His fingers hovered over the keyboard as he scanned through the familiar frames. The marsh, the trees, the occasional movement of reeds swaying in the breeze. But today, it felt different. Every frame carried a weight that wasn't there before.

And then—something flickered on the screen.

Micky leaned in, his heart skipping a beat as the image flashed for just a second, too quick to register clearly. He instinctively reached for the pause button, eyes glued to the screen, but before he could stop the footage, the bell above the door chimed.

Emmett walked in.

Micky's hand jerked, knocking the mouse aside as he turned toward the door. "Sheriff," he greeted, but his voice was tight with distraction, his mind still on what he had just seen.

Emmett gave him a nod, but before he could say a word, Micky's eyes darted back to the monitor. His heart hammered in his chest as he froze, staring at the screen.

A new image had appeared.

Another figure.

For a moment, neither of them spoke. Emmett, noticing Micky's sudden shift in focus, stepped forward, his face tensing with concern. "What is it?"

Micky swallowed hard, his eyes fixed on the monitor. "It's... it's someone else."

Emmett moved closer, glancing at the screen as the chilling realization settled between them. Micky's voice trembled slightly. "It's not just one person out there anymore..."

~ 32 ~

DREAD AT DAWN

The Sheriff and Micky stood motionless, their gazes fixed on the monitor, disbelief carved into their features. Two figures moved cautiously through the thick marsh, barely discernible in the blurry feed from the early morning light filtering through the trees. The sun was climbing, casting long golden beams across the landscape, but it did nothing to relieve the sense of dread. The figures moved in an awkward, disjointed manner, their presence feeling entirely out of place in the quiet of dawn.

The door to Micky's shop groaned open, a bell chiming softly as Preacher John stepped inside, squinting against the harsh daylight flooding the room. Instantly, he sensed the heavy tension lingering between the two men.

"What's going on?" Preacher John asked, his brow furrowing as he noticed their rigid postures and the intense stares locked on the screen.

"There are people in the marsh," Micky replied, his voice tight, tinged with apprehension.

Preacher John shrugged, attempting to shake off the gnawing unease settling in his gut. "It's probably just the new family."

The Sheriff, unusually silent, shook his head firmly. "No. No one's heard from them. I've stopped by twice, and while their car's still there, they aren't."

Micky leaned closer to the monitor, narrowing his eyes at the distorted image. The sunlight streaming through the marsh illuminated everything with a harsh intensity, yet despite the bright day, the scene felt undeniably wrong. "It's definitely someone out there, but they aren't just wandering."

Preacher John's expression shifted, concern etching deeper lines into his face. "But how? I thought you cleared that place, Micky. Didn't you say no spirits remained?"

Micky exhaled, his eyes glued to the screen, his stomach twisting in knots. His thoughts raced, questions swirling in his mind. It wasn't simply about what they were seeing—it was the deeper, unsettling realization that despite everything he believed he knew, he didn't understand what was happening in Devil's Marsh. Micky had witnessed too much over the years—things that most people would dismiss as folklore or superstition, whispered in dark alleys. But this... this was different.

"I'm not talking about spirits this time. These are human."

He said the words, but they felt hollow. Doubt lingered in the recesses of his thoughts, gnawing at him. What if he was wrong? What if there was something more dangerous in the marsh, something that didn't fit into any of the explanations he had come to rely on? Anxiety simmered beneath his calm facade, though he kept his expression composed, unwilling to show Preacher John or the Sheriff the growing fear creeping into his heart.

A heavy stillness descended upon the room, the soft hum of the monitor the only noise as they processed the strange sight on the screen. Preacher John blinked again, the confusion in his eyes slowly turning to alarm. "Human?"

The Sheriff pushed back his chair abruptly, the screech of wood against the floor cutting through the quiet. The sunlight pouring in through the windows offered no comfort against the cold dread that slithered down his spine. "I've got a bad feeling about this."

Even the warmth of the morning outside didn't ease the growing unease inside Micky's shop. Something was wrong—profoundly wrong.

"Let's drive out there, take a look around," the Sheriff said, his voice heavy with worry.

They set off toward Devil's Marsh, the daylight harsh and unyielding as it pierced the trees. Despite the brightness, the swamp felt suffocating. Heat clung to their skin, thick and stifling, as they neared the edge of the marsh. The once-vibrant sounds of birds were abruptly silenced, as though the entire world was holding its breath. The eerie quiet gnawed at their nerves.

When they arrived at the new family's house, the car sat motionless in the driveway, just as the sheriff had mentioned. The home, bathed in daylight, seemed devoid of any life. Too still. They knocked repeatedly, called out, but no one responded. A familiar knot of dread twisted in the Sheriff's gut as he exchanged uneasy glances with Micky and Preacher John. Something wasn't right.

They trudged into the marsh, their boots sinking into the mud with every step. The morning sun filtered through the trees, casting long rays of light, yet the atmosphere felt thick, oppressive. With each step, it seemed as if the marsh was closing in on them, threatening to swallow them whole.

Then, near a twisted old tree, something caught the light.

"Over here," the sheriff rasped, his voice rough. He knelt down, cold dread washing over him in waves. He reached for the object, and his stomach clenched. It was a license plate—Izzy's, half-buried in the muck.

Micky's chest tightened. "Izzy..." he murmured, the weight of the moment crashing down on him. Regret, guilt, and something darker flooded his thoughts—the crushing realization that he had failed her. She wasn't just another name on a list of disappearances; she was someone he cared about, someone who had placed her trust in him. His throat tightened as the truth sank in—Izzy wasn't coming back. And it had happened under his watch.

"We need more people out here," the Sheriff muttered, already reaching for his radio. "This isn't right."

Hours later, the Sheriff's team combed through the swamp. As the sun climbed higher, the temperature became unbearable, making the air thick and heavy. The oppressive silence remained, amplifying their unease. Eventually, they located Izzy's car, sunken deep into the marsh, swallowed by the earth itself. There was no sign of Izzy. The sight was nightmarish, like something out of a twisted horror story.

Micky stared at the submerged vehicle, his mind racing. His hand trembled as he dialed Donna's number. For a moment, he hesitated, thumb hovering over the screen, imagining how this news would shatter her. Donna and Izzy had been like sisters. Breaking the news wasn't just delivering bad news; it was crushing a soul.

"Donna," Micky whispered, his voice trembling. "I've got some bad news. It's about Izzy... She didn't make it out of the marsh."

The pause on the other end of the call felt like it lasted forever. When Donna finally spoke, her voice cracked, barely above a whisper. "She's... gone?"

Micky swallowed the lump in his throat. "I'm so sorry, Donna."

As he ended the call, a weight pressed down on his chest. His thoughts spiraled out of control.

Preacher John stood a few steps away, staring into the murky depths of the marsh. His shoulders sagged under the weight of everything that had happened, the suffocating silence of the swamp making it all feel even heavier. "I feel like I failed her," he whispered, the words barely escaping his lips.

Micky, still reeling from the conversation with Donna, didn't respond at first. His mind raced with memories of Izzy, of all the things he should have done differently. After a moment, he finally muttered, "Me too."

Preacher John turned, meeting Micky's eyes. He saw the pain and self-blame written clearly on his friend's face. "You did everything you could," Preacher John said softly, trying to reassure him. "You protected her from the evil in that house. How could we have known that not only were we dealing with the supernatural, but with something human, too?"

Micky swallowed hard, his fists clenched by his sides. "I should've seen it coming, John. All those signs... I thought I was facing something from the other side, something beyond this world. But this..." He trailed off, the weight of the truth settling deeper in his chest.

Preacher John shook his head. "No one could've known. We were ready for spirits, for curses, for all the strange things we've dealt with in this place. But this? We weren't prepared for something like this—something human."

Back in town, rumors spread like wildfire. Bayou Vista buzzed with fearful whispers, residents too scared to openly acknowledge the growing terror. The family's disappearance, combined with Izzy's vanishing, sent shockwaves through the tight-knit community. What if something from the marsh had been responsible for the missing women all these years?

Later that afternoon, Loretta walked into Micky's shop. The familiar jingle of the bell over the door rang out, but it did little to ease the tension in her chest. Her heart pounded as she stepped inside, her fingers trembling slightly as she pushed the door closed behind her.

Micky, sitting behind the counter, looked up and immediately saw the unease in her eyes. She walked over to him slowly, as if carrying the weight of her past with each step. Her voice was shaky, barely above a whisper, as she finally spoke. "Micky... do you think it could be him? The clown? The one who grabbed me that night when I was ten?"

Micky hesitated, burdened by his own fears. He didn't want to believe it, but he couldn't dismiss the possibility. "No," he said slowly. "I don't think it was him, Loretta. We never proved it was Roy or Gary, though."

Loretta's gaze sharpened. "But what if it's still out there? What if it's him?"

Her voice trembled, and Micky noticed something new—Loretta had been quiet for years, but now, a darker fear seemed to have surfaced. He wondered if the nightmares had returned, or if something had stirred her memory.

"There's been talk," Loretta whispered, "about an ancient spirit... something guarding the swamp. Rosie mentioned it once. I thought she was just being paranoid, but now... I'm not sure."

Micky chuckled nervously, though the unease in his chest didn't lift. "Rosie's a cheeky woman, Loretta. You can't believe everything she says."

But even as he spoke, a chill snaked down his spine. Could Rosie have been telling the truth all those years ago? Micky's smile faltered, and Loretta caught the brief flicker of doubt in his eyes.

Later that evening, after the town had fallen silent, Micky stood at the window, gazing out into the deserted street. His hands trembled as his mind spun with unanswered questions. Something felt off. The sensation of being watched crept over him, wrapping around him like a cold, invisible hand.

His eyes darted to the corner of the room, but nothing moved. Still, the feeling lingered—a frigid, creeping presence hovering just out of sight. A faint creak from the back room made the hair on the back of his neck stand up. He froze, straining to hear any other sound. Was it a footstep? Or was it all in his head?

Micky turned back to the window, and for a brief moment, he thought he saw a figure standing at the edge of the street, beyond the glow of the streetlights. His heart thudded in his chest, breath catching in his throat.

But when he blinked, the figure was gone.

Micky pressed his forehead against the cool glass, fogging it with his breath. His shop, once a refuge, now felt strange, foreign. The walls seemed to pulse with an energy he couldn't explain, and his thoughts kept circling back to the marsh, to Izzy, to the endless questions that gnawed at him.

What—or who—was really out there?

Micky shuddered, trying to shake the feeling, but deep down, he knew. Something had been watching him.

And it wouldn't stay hidden much longer.

~ 33 ~

THE LABLANC FAMILY

Micky sat hunched over his desk in the dim light of his shop, the journal lying open in front of him, its worn pages filled with haunting scrawls. His fingers traced the jagged lines of text, his eyes scanning the faded ink for the truth he so desperately needed.

Today, he would find out who—or what—Billy LaBlanc really was. Billy wasn't just a name that had appeared in stories whispered around the marsh. He was the son of Mary LaBlanc, a name that had been buried deep in the history of the land for generations. His family had been rooted in Bayou Vista for as long as the town had existed, their bloodlines tied to the very earth. And now, Micky was beginning to understand why the LaBlanc family was so feared.

As Micky flipped through the journal's brittle pages, his heart raced. He had seen enough to know that something terrible had been happening in Devil's Marsh for centuries. The journal described dark rituals, ancient rites carried out by the LaBlanc family—rituals that required the blood of the innocent. Women and children, sacrificed to something older than anyone could comprehend. The purpose was clear: power, control, and most horrifying of all, a twisted form of immortality. Billy LaBlanc wasn't just a man lost to the past. He had been part of it—part of the evil that had festered in the marsh for generations.

Micky's stomach turned as he read on, the details more grotesque with every sentence. The sacrifices weren't quick deaths. They were drawn out, ritualistic offerings to the marsh itself, carried out in hopes of gaining eternal life. And the painted faces—the clowns—they weren't stories invented to scare children. The clowns were real. The grotesque makeup marked those who had been claimed by the rituals, their souls twisted into something unrecognizable.

"Jesus," Micky muttered under his breath, the bile rising in his throat. His hand instinctively reached for the monitor. He knew he had to check the footage from the marsh. Maybe there was something—anything—that could make sense of what was happening —but nothing was there.

Micky couldn't sit in the shop any longer. The air felt too thick, too oppressive. He needed to clear his head, figure out what to do next. Grabbing his jacket, he slipped out the door and headed toward *Tanya's Crawfish Shack*, hoping the familiar sounds of clinking plates and low murmurs would give him a moment of peace.

The walk through Bayou Vista was quiet, too quiet. The town had been on edge ever since Izzy's disappearance, and now the unsettling truth about the LaBlanc family twisted in Micky's mind like a knife. He shoved his hands deep into his pockets as he walked, the chill in the air doing little to shake off the sense of dread that clung to him.

When he pushed open the door to Tanya's, the familiar scent of seafood and spices wrapped around him, though today, even that comfort felt distant.

"Hey there, Micky," Tanya called from behind the counter, wiping her hands. "Crazy weather we've been having, huh?"

"Blistering hot during the day, and freezing at night," Micky replied, managing a small, tired grin.

Tanya chuckled softly. "Ain't that the truth. Have a seat—I'll be right with you."

Micky's gaze shifted to Gail, Patricia, and Shannon sitting by the window. They waved him over, but the usual warmth was missing from their smiles. They'd heard about Izzy.

Micky forced a smile as he sat down, but his thoughts were still swirling with the two images that had led him to the marsh the day before.

"I'm glad to see you," Gail said, her eyes searching Micky's face for any hint of what he might be holding back. "We were worried about you."

Micky shrugged, picking up the menu as a way to avoid their gazes. "I'm alright. Just... tired."

Shannon frowned, leaning in slightly. "Tired? Micky, you look like you've seen a ghost. And considering what's been going on around here... that's saying something."

Patricia nodded. "Have you heard anything more about Izzy? It's been days now, and everyone's talking. People are saying she just vanished. Like, out of thin air."

Micky set the menu down, his fingers drumming against the table. He wanted to tell them everything, about the journal, about what he'd seen on the monitor. But how could he? How could he explain that Izzy had become something else, twisted by the same darkness that had claimed so many before her?

"She didn't just disappear," Micky said quietly, his eyes fixed on the table. "Something took her."

Gail's eyes widened. "What do you mean 'something'? Are you talking about the marsh?"

Micky hesitated, then nodded. "It's... complicated. There's more to this than just someone going missing. I've been looking into it, and... I think the marsh, or something in it, is involved."

Shannon shivered. "That marsh has always given me the creeps. I never trusted it. Preacher John said that her car was found in the swamp. Is that true?"

Before Micky could respond, the door swung open, and Rosie swaggered in, her eyes immediately locking on their table. She smirked, making her way over, and leaned against the back of Micky's chair.

"Well, well, look who's here," she said, her voice dripping with sarcasm. "The man who's always sticking his nose in things better left alone."

Micky clenched his jaw but didn't respond. He wasn't in the mood for Rosie's games.

Rosie chuckled. "I heard about Izzy. Shame, really. But I'm not surprised."

Micky turned his head slightly, glancing up at her. "How did you know something was coming for her, Rosie? You mentioned it before."

Rosie's smirk faded slightly, her eyes darkening. "Once you've been there, Micky, they don't let you go. Izzy was always marked. It was just a matter of time."

The table fell silent, tension thick in the air. Patricia shifted uncomfortably in her seat, her eyes darting between Micky and Rosie.

Gail leaned forward, her voice barely above a whisper. "What are you talking about? What do you mean 'marked'?"

Rosie's lips curled into a mocking smile. "You all think you know this town, this place. But you don't. The marsh takes what it wants, and once you're part of it, there's no escaping. Izzy didn't just wander into that place by accident. She was called."

Micky's fists tightened under the table, anger bubbling up inside him. He didn't want to believe Rosie, but the truth was staring him in the face.

"Called by who?" Micky asked, his voice cold.

Rosie leaned in closer, her voice low and menacing. "By the same thing that's been watching you, Micky. You've felt it, haven't you?"

The words sent a chill down Micky's spine, but before he could respond, Tanya bustled over, her cheerful voice cutting through the tension. Rosie straightened up, smirking at Micky as she pushed back from the table. "You'll see soon enough," she said with a sly grin, turning on her heel and walking away without another word.

Tanya's lively energy seemed out of place in the heavy atmosphere Rosie had left behind, but she offered a brief reprieve from the unsettling conversation.

"Hey there, folks! What can I get for y'all tonight?" Tanya asked, her bright smile doing little to ease the weight in the air.

"We're just about ready," Gail said, forcing a smile as she glanced at the menu. "You've got to try the special, Micky."

Micky nodded absently, his mind still on Rosie's words. He could feel the weight of the journal in his bag, as though it were pulling him back to the shop, to the dark truths that lay hidden in its pages. But right now, he had to sit, had to pretend like things were normal, even though he knew they were anything but.

As they placed their orders, the conversations turned to more mundane topics—work, the weather, the new family that had moved into town. But the undercurrent of fear never left the table. Patricia couldn't help but glance over her shoulder now and then, as though she expected something or someone to appear at any moment.

After Tanya left with their orders, Gail leaned in closer to Micky. "Do you really think it's the marsh? I mean, all these people going missing, it can't be a coincidence."

Micky sighed, running a hand through his hair. "It's not just the marsh, Gail. It's what's in it."

Shannon shuddered. "What do we do, Micky?"

Micky shook his head. "I don't know, Shannon. I wish I had the answers."

Rosie's words echoed in his mind—*they don't let you go.* He knew now, more than ever, that whatever was happening in Devil's Marsh, it was far from over.

Just then, Firecracker, known for her fiery personality, and Taylor stopped by the table, their faces lighting up as they saw Micky. "Hey, Micky," Firecracker said with a warm smile. "We've been worried about you. It's good to see you out."

Taylor nodded in agreement. "Yeah, nice to see you."

They shared a few pleasantries before heading to their own table.

As the dinner conversation carried on, Micky's mind wandered back to the monitor in his shop. He knew he had to check the footage from the marsh. Maybe there was something—anything—that could make sense of what was happening. Maybe he had missed something, some crucial clue hidden in the frames.

Excusing himself from the table, he hurried back to his shop, his footsteps quickening as the sense of dread tightened around him. When he reached the shop, the familiar jingle of the doorbell sent a shiver down his spine.

He rushed to the back, his fingers flying over the keyboard as he brought up the footage. His pulse quickened as the screen flickered to life, showing the marsh once again. At first, it looked the same—silent, waiting. But something felt wrong, something unsettling stirred within him.

Then, it happened—movement.

Leaning closer, Micky gripped the edge of the desk, his breath catching in his throat. Two figures appeared on the screen, barely visible at first but growing clearer as they passed through the trees. His stomach twisted as he stared at the first figure—a woman—her face twisted, a grotesque mix of life and death. The eerie makeup distorted her features, turning her into something from a nightmare. Her eyes, cold and vacant, stared straight ahead, and her jerky, unnatural movements sent a chill down Micky's spine.

Behind her, a second figure stepped out of the shadows. A tall, gaunt man, his presence alone filled Micky with dread. But he knew—this wasn't Billy. It couldn't be. The spirits had been laid to rest. Whatever this was, it was something else, something darker.

The man led the woman, his steps deliberate, as if guiding her deeper into the marsh. Micky's heart raced, his mind whirling in confusion. What had he just seen?

Suddenly, the bell above the door jingled, shattering the silence. Micky's heart leapt into his throat as he whipped around toward the entrance. The shop was empty. The door hadn't opened.

Breathing heavily, he turned back to the monitor, but the figures were gone. Panic set in as he frantically scrubbed through the footage, his hands trembling. The marsh was empty, the scene erased. Had it all been in his mind?

The door behind him creaked, and the bell jingled again. Micky froze, his blood turning to ice. That unsettling sensation of being watched gripped him tighter than ever.

Slowly, he turned toward the door, his heart hammering in his chest. The shop remained empty, the stillness suffocating.

His eyes darted back to the monitor, the sense of unease growing stronger. Then, there she was again—the woman. Her slow, stiff movements seemed unnatural as she walked through the marsh. The light from the moon caught her face just enough to reveal the horrifying truth—her face was painted. White makeup smeared across her skin, with jagged streaks of red slashed across her lips, forming a twisted, grotesque smile.

Micky's chest tightened as recognition hit him like a punch to the gut. That walk, that auburn hair, that face... His breath caught, and in a hushed whisper, he uttered, "Izzy?"

~ 34 ~

A NEW EVIL

Early the next day, Micky sat in his shop, his hands trembling slightly as he thumbed through the worn, yellowed pages of Mary LaBlanc's journal. The dim light from the desk lamp cast a sickly glow on the pages, making the cryptic handwriting even harder to decipher. He had looked through the footage from last night, ready to show the Sheriff and Preacher John what he had seen. But the footage showed nothing—just an empty marsh, still and silent. No figures. No answers.

His heart pounded in his chest as he returned to the journal. The truth had to be inside these pages. The journal wasn't just a collection of strange tales and cryptic notes. It was a warning—one that Micky now realized had gone ignored for far too long.

Micky's eyes skimmed over the shaky handwriting, the faded ink making the cryptic symbols seem to dance on the page. His thoughts were scattered, but something caught his attention—something he had missed before.

He leaned closer, brow furrowed in concentration. Mary had written about Billy, her son. About how the evil in the marsh had consumed him. She spoke of how his sister had tried to flee from the shadows that clung to their family, terrified and confused.

But then Micky found it—the passage that made his blood run cold.

Mary had written about a baby.

His hands trembled as he read further:

I tried to take the baby to the marsh to sacrifice it, but Billy wouldn't let me. He told me if anything ever happened to that child, he would kill me.

Micky's breath hitched. *The baby is still alive.*

It was all right there, in Mary's twisted account. The LaBlanc family wasn't just cursed by the marsh. The curse ran deeper—it was in their blood.

Micky's eyes widened as he continued reading:

Billy and his sister had sinned. And their son, Micah... he walks in the shadows. He belongs to the marsh.

The realization hit Micky like a punch to the gut. Micah was still alive. The baby, the product of something twisted and unnatural, was not only real—he was out there. Walking, breathing, living among them, tied to the dark power of the marsh.

Micky's heart pounded as he leaned back in his chair, the journal slipping from his fingers. If Micah was alive, then everything they had thought about the marsh—the disappearances, the strange occurrences, the evil—pointed back to him.

The weight of it all felt unbearable. Micky couldn't stay in the shop any longer. He grabbed his jacket, pushed his chair back, and stormed out. There was one person who knew more about the town's dark past than anyone—Rosie Fontenot. She was always at the library this time of day, digging through old records, piecing together stories most people would rather forget.

Micky arrived at the library, its usual brightness welcoming, a stark contrast to the darkness weighing on his mind. The place was alive with the quiet hum of activity—patrons flipping through books, students typing away at laptops, and the occasional sound of laughter drifting from the children's section. But even in the midst of the library's familiar bustle, Micky felt a growing sense of unease.

He spotted Rosie in her usual corner, her back to the rest of the room, flipping through a stack of old records. She was deep in thought, as usual, her fingers running over the worn pages of a book, her eyes scanning the text as if searching for something long forgotten.

Micky approached, pulling out a chair. "Rosie, I need your help."

Without looking up, Rosie smirked. "Help with what? Thought you didn't believe in all this old town gossip."

Micky sat down across from her, the urgency clear in his voice. "It's about the marsh. And... Micah."

At the mention of the name, Rosie's smirk faded. She set the book down and leaned back in her chair. "Ah, Micah. Didn't think you'd come around to that one."

"You know about him?" Micky pressed, his hands resting uneasily on the table.

Rosie's gaze grew more serious. "People have been whispering about him for years. Ever since Billy and his sister... well, let's just say the LaBlanc family had secrets. Secrets that run deeper than most folks care to admit."

Micky swallowed, his throat tight. "Is he alive?"

Rosie glanced around, making sure no one was listening. "The marsh takes what it wants, Micky. Some souls it keeps, some it spits out. Micah... he wasn't supposed to survive. But I've heard enough to know he walks with the marsh's blessing—if you can call it that."

Micky leaned in, his voice tense. "Has anyone ever seen him?"

Rosie let out a sharp, dry laugh, unsettling in its coldness. "If you do, you won't be able to tell anyone—because you'll be dead," she said, her eyes glinting with a grim mix of warning and amusement.

A knot of dread tightened in Micky's stomach as the weight of her words sank in.

Rosie's tone shifted, her expression growing serious. "Well, you know all about souls, don't you? Look who I'm talking to. No one ever mentioned him to you before?"

"No," Micky replied, his voice steady but laced with curiosity.

"Well, personally, I think the old lady killed him—that's why she's dead," Rosie smirked briefly, but the humor quickly drained from her face. "Not too many folks remember the baby. The rumors always circled around Billy, his daddy," she murmured, her voice dropping to a near whisper. "But wherever that bastard is, the marsh is never far behind."

Micky opened his mouth to respond, but Rosie waved him off dismissively. "Whatever, Micky," she said, her tone sharp. "Piss off now. I got more research to do."

Micky chuckled to himself, shaking his head, wondering how long Rosie had been waiting to tell him to piss off. He knew her well enough to recognize the impatience behind her sharp dismissal. As he turned to leave, he glanced back one last time, watching as Rosie dove right back into her books, already absorbed in whatever secrets she was hunting for in the dusty pages.

Later that evening, Micky returned to his shop, his mind swirling with Rosie's words. He felt like he was living in a nightmare, one he couldn't wake up from. The journal, the disappearances—all of it pointed to the same conclusion: Micah was the key. But to what?

He couldn't sit still. His thoughts raced as he paced the shop, the weight of everything bearing down on him. Then, as he leafed through the journal again, a new line caught his eye, one scrawled in hurried handwriting, as if it were a final warning:

The marsh follows Micah, and where he goes, the darkness spreads. But he doesn't know. Not yet.

Micky's breath caught in his throat. *Micah is the key.* But did Micah even understand the power he held? And if he did, what was he planning?

A knot formed in Micky's stomach. He glanced at the monitor—the one connected to the camera in the marsh. His fingers twitched as he rewound the footage, desperate to find some trace of the figures he had seen the night before. But the screen was blank. Nothing moved. No sign of the woman, no sign of the man.

Suddenly, a face appeared on the screen, staring directly into the camera.

Micky froze, his blood turning to ice.

The face was gaunt, pale, with dark, hollow eyes. Micky's breath caught as he glanced between the screen and the old photograph of Billy LaBlanc and his family, tucked in his desk drawer. His hands fumbled for the photo, holding it up beside the image on the screen. The same eyes. The same hollow, haunting gaze.

His hands shook. *Is this Micah?* Micky's mind raced. *Had Izzy been seeing Micah instead of Billy?*

The questions clawed at him, but before he could make sense of it, a noise outside the shop jolted him back to the present. A slow, creaking sound, like someone—or something—moving just beyond the door.

Micky's heart thundered in his chest. He grabbed the shotgun from behind the counter, gripping it tightly as he approached the door, his every nerve on edge. He peered through the window, the cold night air pressing against the glass.

Nothing. The street was empty. But the feeling of being watched clung to him, suffocating.

Slowly, cautiously, he unlocked the door and stepped outside. The night was eerily silent, the town bathed in an unsettling stillness. Micky scanned the street, his heart pounding in his ears, but there was no sign of life.

And yet, that feeling remained.

He turned to go back inside, but as he reached for the door, a figure stepped into view, emerging from the shadows across the street.

Micky's breath caught in his throat. The figure stood motionless, bathed in the pale glow of the moonlight. His face was hidden, but his posture, his presence—it sent a wave of terror crashing over Micky.

"Micah?"

Micky's hand froze on the doorknob, his pulse hammering in his ears. The figure remained still, watching, waiting.

The town was silent, but in the distance, Micky could feel the marsh—alive, waiting, feeding on the darkness.

And now, it had sent its son...

Dear Readers,

Thank you for choosing to read Devil's Marsh! I hope you enjoyed the journey as much as I loved bringing it to life. If you'd like to stay updated on all my upcoming releases or even have the chance to become a character in one of my stories, be sure to follow my Facebook page. I truly enjoy connecting with my readers and hearing your thoughts, so feel free to reach out and say hello!

facebook.com/AuthorCarolACampbellGhostStories

or you can email me:
authorcarola.campbell@hotmail.com

I hope you enjoyed Devil's Marsh as much as I loved writing it! If the story resonated with you, I'd be truly grateful if you could take a moment to leave a review. Your thoughts mean the world to me, and your support helps other readers discover my books. Thank you for being part of this journey, and I can't wait to hear what you think!

Thanks!
Carol